Christmas is

Gifts are not a̲ͭͤ hold in your hand̲s̲. The gift we celebrate at Christmas is that small baby born in a stable, though the shepherds and the wise men did manage to bring presents as well.

These books also celebrate Christmas, and each deals with a different gift, the kind that can bring immeasurable love and contentment down the years— which we wish for all of you.

Enjoy!

Jessica Matthews's interest in medicine began at a young age, and she nourished it with medical stories and hospital-based television programmes. After a stint as a teenage candy-striper, she pursued a career as a clinical laboratory scientist. When not writing or on duty she fills her day with countless family and school-related activities. Jessica lives in the central United States with her husband, daughter and son.

Recent titles by the same author:

PRESCRIPTIONS AND PROMISES
HIS MADE-TO-ORDER BRIDE

LISA'S CHRISTMAS ASSIGNMENT

BY
JESSICA MATTHEWS

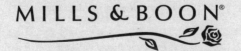

All the characters in this book have no existence outside the imagination of the author, and have no relation whatsoever to anyone bearing the same name or names. They are not even distantly inspired by any individual known or unknown to the author, and all the incidents are pure invention.

First published in Great Britain 2000
Harlequin Mills & Boon Limited,
Eton House, 18-24 Paradise Road, Richmond, Surrey TW9 1SR

© Jessica Matthews 2000

ISBN 0 263 82276 1

Set in Times Roman 10½ on 12 pt.
03-1200-46566

Printed and bound in Spain
by Litografia Rosés, S.A., Barcelona

CHAPTER ONE

How *did* 007 keep his cool in situations like these?

Lisa Mallory cautiously poked her head out of the staff lounge and cast furtive glances in both directions. Avoiding her colleagues was more difficult than she'd imagined. James Bond made slinking around unnoticed appear so easy but, then, he'd had years of practice.

Some might say she was being melodramatic in her attempt to leave the building, but taking her lumps for missing a staff meeting seemed easier than suffering through today's agenda with a smile pasted on her face.

The coast was clear.

She tiptoed to the intersecting hallway and stopped to check again. If she made it past Alice's office without being seen, she'd be home free.

Just as she was ready to take off, the sound of voices warned her to plant her feet firmly on the tile floor. A surreptitious peek revealed her friend and fellow practice nurse, Savanna Gibson, walking alongside Roger Maguire, one of the physician assistants. Although she wasn't worried if Savanna caught a glimpse of her on her way out the building, Roger would sound the alarm.

She froze.

'Did you tell Lisa about the meeting?' Roger asked, his dark coloring contrasting with Savanna's fair-haired Norwegian bloodlines.

'She knows, but I think she's running late,' Savanna replied, her strides matching her companion's.

Thank you, thank you, Lisa silently told her friend. I owe you one.

'She'd better show up,' Roger threatened, although everyone knew his bark was worse than his bite. 'If we have to endure Alice's sessions, so does she. If I remember right, Lisa managed to escape the last one.'

'Keeping score?' Savanna teased.

'You bet. If one of us has to suffer, we *all* have to suffer,' he grumbled as they disappeared into Alice Carmichael's office.

As the Farmington Medical Clinic's office manager, Alice took her duties seriously. Communication was her watchword and she made it her personal mission to be sure the staff was well informed on every detail, which meant weekly meetings. Nearly everyone agreed that the majority of issues didn't warrant more than a brief memo, explaining the changes, but Alice refused to rely on what she considered a risky method of exchanging information.

Everyone rued the day she'd attended a seminar on communication and employee productivity.

Lisa poised herself to move on the count of five. Just as she reached four, a breath of air on the back of her neck sent a shiver down her spine. Before she could react, a distinctly masculine whisper spoke directly in her ear.

'Spying on someone in particular?'

Lisa nearly jumped out of her skin. She whirled around to face her immediate boss, Dr Simon Travers. Since he towered over her, her nose came to the level of his shoulder. 'You scared me to death.'

'Sorry,' he said, keeping his voice low. 'I don't mean to be rude, but what *are* you doing?'

'I'm trying to go home.'

His gaze landed on her knee-length wool coat. 'So I see.

But do you always go through the stealth routine in order to leave? If so, we must be working you too hard.'

Lisa's face warmed. 'It's not that at all.'

The corners of his mouth twitched and she had the feeling he was laughing at her. 'A spy-in-training, perhaps?'

'Of course not.' Her whisper sounded waspish. 'Can we, *please*, discuss this another time? I really want to get out of here without being caught.'

Although his dark brown eyes held traces of curiosity, he didn't say a word. Instead, he moved in front of her to shield her from anyone who might come upon them unawares. Standing behind him on tiptoe, she pressed in close enough to inhale the faint scent of antiseptic soap and a tangy men's cologne.

Oddly enough, hiding behind him was a rather comforting experience. In fact, she was somewhat surprised that he'd helped her without asking more questions. After all, he had nothing to gain or lose, one way or the other.

Minutes ticked by and her toes began to cramp. She shifted positions to relieve the pain, but her balance wobbled. Eager to regain her footing, she placed one hand on the lightly textured pale blue wall and the other in the middle of Simon's broad back.

The warmth under her palm sent tingles up her arm and a shudder of pleasure down her spine. Surprised by the strength of the sensation, she abruptly dropped her hand. It couldn't have anything to do with Simon, could it? She'd rubbed elbows, so to speak, with him for months and hadn't experienced anything quite like this before.

He turned his head, a question written on his face as if he'd felt something, too. Lisa gulped, forced a tremulous smile, then whispered a terse, 'Sorry.'

Fortunately, he didn't say a word, only nodded an acknowledgement, while she contemplated the reason for her

unusual reaction. Static electricity and nerves, she decided.
Her fear of discovery—the adrenalin rush of danger—had
merely heightened her senses and made her jumpy. That
was all.

Placated by her own explanation, she waited for his sig-
nal. As soon as he motioned her forward, Lisa darted for
the door leading to the parking lot.

Conscious of him following on her heels, she didn't stop
until she breathed in the crisp November air.

She faced him. 'Thanks.'

Simon shrugged his shoulders. Funny how they appeared
so much larger in his sports coat than in his usual white
lab jacket. 'No problem.'

'I should explain—,' she began.

'You don't have to,' he said.

'I want to,' she insisted. 'Especially since I made you an
accessory.'

A small smile tugged at his mouth. 'Accomplices should
know what's going on, I suppose. Although you don't seem
like the lawbreaker type.'

'Alice will disagree when I don't attend her meeting,'
she commented ruefully. 'She takes her sessions seriously
and expects everyone else to do the same. I don't normally
miss them, but I couldn't stand the thought of listening to
today's topic.'

'Really? What did she have on the agenda?'

Lisa hated to admit her reasons. They sounded rather
childish, but she owed him that much. 'I really shouldn't
tell you, but it concerns Christmas.'

'Christmas?'

His blank look prompted her to explain. 'You know.
Christmas. Parties. Gifts. The whole nine yards.'

'Ah, Christmas,' he said knowingly.

'Christmas is a wonderful holiday,' she hurried to add,

noticing how the wind blew his straight russet-colored hair into mild disarray. Somehow it made him seem more human than he'd ever appeared in the six months since he'd joined the Farmington Medical Clinic. 'I just don't enjoy the fuss everyone makes during this time of year.'

'You don't owe me any explanations,' he said as his gaze intently searched her face. 'I understand.'

'You do?' He was probably the only one in the entire world who did. Other than her family, of course, and they didn't count.

He nodded. 'I know other people who feel the same way. Now, if you don't want to undo our efforts, I suggest you hurry on home before someone looks out the window.'

Lisa liked the way he said 'our'. It implied a kinship that she didn't find disturbing. Not one bit.

'You're right. I'd better go.' She skirted his Dodge Intrepid to reach her black Toyota Avalon. 'Thanks again.'

He waved at her before he folded himself inside his vehicle. Lisa drove away, conscious of his car trailing hers for several blocks before he turned onto a side street, presumably toward home.

The neighborhood was middle class and the houses average-sized. As a bachelor, she'd pictured him living in one of the newer apartment complexes that catered to high-income singles. A modest three-bedroom home didn't seem to fit but, then, mystery surrounded the clinic's newest physician.

Last May he'd replaced a family practitioner, who'd moved to the city, and had brought their medical group consisting of a surgeon, a pediatrician, an internist, a family practice specialist, a nurse practitioner and two physician's assistants to full staff. He was a quiet man—very different from the bubbly Wendy Unruh who'd left for greener pastures.

Having enjoyed working with Dr Unruh, she'd considered herself fortunate to fall into the same comfortable routine with her replacement. Like Lisa, Dr Travers valued his privacy and she refused to encroach upon what she considered forbidden territory.

Right now, though, she had a lot of questions about her boss and no answers. Not many understood her feelings about Christmas, but he did and she wanted to know why.

Mind your own business, she told herself. As long as they had a comfortable professional relationship, what more could she ask for?

All she'd craved had been peace and quiet. From the way the morning had gone, Lisa should have known that peace and quiet were the last things she'd enjoy this noon hour.

She tensed as Alice marched into the conference room, wearing a satisfied smirk on her thin, sixty-year-old face. Her sensible pumps made dull thuds on the carpeted floor and added to the pounding at Lisa's temples.

'You're a hard woman to find,' Alice commented conversationally.

'Just keeping busy,' Lisa answered, wondering if she should try to hide the evidence of her transgression before Alice added this strike to the one Lisa had earned yesterday.

The decision instantly flew out of her control as Alice's gaze landed on the table.

Her mouth turned into a disapproving line as she obviously caught sight of Lisa's half-eaten sandwich on top of a pile of patient folders. One perfectly drawn midnight black eyebrow arched upward.

'Eating?' She yanked a chair away from the table and perched on the edge of the seat cushion. Alice ran the office with the energy of a whirlwind but, regardless of her activities, spots and wrinkles never appeared on her clothes. They didn't dare.

Well aware of Alice's rules for neatness in the conference room, especially if the doctors had scheduled a meeting in it for later in the day, Lisa braced herself for a lecture. Although she understood the manager's viewpoint—their lounge often looked like a disaster area—she thought Alice carried her edict to the extreme.

Still, Alice possessed enough other good qualities and organizational skills to make one willing to overlook, or at least to tolerate, this particular idiosyncrasy.

'I needed to catch up on some of my paperwork. The lounge was too crowded so I came here,' Lisa said. Alice only accepted excuses if they were of the catastrophic variety. Nursing her headache in solitude wouldn't influence the manager in the slightest.

Alice's dark eyes took on a thoughtful gleam. 'Maybe we should stagger our lunch-hours. I can make a schedule and post it—'

'That isn't necessary,' Lisa hastily interrupted, visualizing a list of assigned times for individual staff members to use their break room. The game of circumventing Alice could turn nasty and develop into all-out war. Roger already chafed under most of her dictates and wouldn't accept additional ones with kindness.

'In any case, I'll leave this place spotless before I go. I promise.'

Alice sniffed. 'Be sure you do.'

Before Lisa could feel relief, Alice pressed on. 'But that's not why I'm looking for you. We have to deal with something far more important.'

Lisa tensed. Alice only had private talks with staff if they'd received a complaint. She tried to think of a recently dissatisfied patient and drew a blank. 'What's wrong?'

'Nothing. You and I need to talk about Christmas.'

Lisa groaned inwardly. She'd have preferred discussing any topic other than the holiday season. Apparently it was time to pay the proverbial piper for yesterday's misdeed. 'We do?'

Alice nodded. 'Absolutely. Great events don't just happen. They're *planned*. November will fly by, and before we know it it'll be December.'

'But—'

Alice held up her hands. 'Some people don't classify Christmas as a great event, but a lot of us do. So we need to organize our party now.'

Lisa gathered the notes she'd been recording and inserted them in the appropriate area of the folder. 'Whatever you decided at the meeting is fine with me.'

'I'm not asking for your opinion. I need your input.'

'I can't imagine for what. Your parties are the greatest. No one can possibly top them.'

Alice preened under Lisa's well-meant praise. 'Thank you, but we *did* miss you last night. Apparently, you forgot to mark our gathering on your calendar.'

A glint appeared in the older woman's eyes as if she knew more details than she was divulging.

Lisa smiled weakly. 'I appreciate you wanting my suggestions, but I'll go along with whatever the group decides.'

To Lisa, holiday parties ranked alongside root canals in the favorite-activities department, although she hadn't always felt that way. Last year, her Christmas wedding plans had fallen apart after Bryan had admitted loving someone else. Those weeks before the ceremony which should have been hers had been sheer misery and she'd made it through by counting the days until December 26th.

The pain should have lessened this year, but it hadn't. Bryan's announcement of his wife's pregnancy had started the tongues wagging at full speed. If another person patted her shoulder and sympathized, Lisa would scream.

She was tired of people attributing her unattached state to still being in love with her childhood sweetheart. It was untrue, of course, but without a male appearing steadily in her life she couldn't put those rumors to rest. Because she hadn't met anyone she cared to spend her evenings with, she'd opted to combat the gossip by doing something unusual, exciting and completely different during this holiday season.

She was taking a Christmas cruise.

She'd saved her money, planned her trip and bought her ticket. All she needed to do was pick up her passes from the travel agent, expand her wardrobe with several eye-catching outfits and purchase tons of sunscreen.

'I'm glad you're so open-minded, because we voted for you to take on a very important responsibility.'

Lisa should have known Alice's smug smile didn't bode well for her. 'You did?' She hadn't talked to Savanna since yesterday morning. Apparently her friend had some explaining to do.

Alice didn't bat an eyelid. 'Actually, Roger and Savanna suggested the idea and we all thought it a marvelous one.'

Vowing to get even with them both, Lisa managed a weak smile.

'As you know, we've worked hard this year to raise money for the doctors' gifts and have a sizeable amount to spend.'

Lisa nodded. Everyone had agreed to donate cans of coffee and the money charged per cup went into the clinic's Christmas fund. From this, the experienced gamblers in the group bought a lottery ticket with the understanding that any cash earned would also be added to their fund. The ticket had been a winner and their small account had instantly mushroomed.

'At our meeting, we thought of presents for all of our doctors,' Alice continued, 'except for Dr Travers. Your mission is to find out what he would like and/or need.'

Lisa leaned back in her chair, overwhelmed and incredulous. Apparently her James-Bond-type maneouvre was coming back to haunt her with a vengeance. 'How am I going to do that?'

'I'm sure you'll think of a way.'

'Surely someone else could—'

'You're his nurse,' Alice broke in. 'You're around him all day long. Surely you have some ideas about his hobbies and interests.'

Hobbies? Interests? As far as Lisa knew, the man lived in a total vacuum. 'Well, I don't. SueEllen loves to talk. Assign her the job. She loves a challenge.'

Alice shook her head. 'I realize your receptionist can convince a clam to open up, but she's tried. Says he's impossible.'

Lisa wasn't surprised. She knew only the bare minimum about the doctor—he was almost thirty, single and had one sister, a niece and a nephew. Although she faithfully asked about his weekends each Monday morning, he always responded with the same monosyllabic reply. He never volunteered any details and either smoothly changed the subject to something work-related or stared at her as if he could peer into her very soul.

But now Alice wanted her to quiz him on his habits, hobbies and preferences. The idea sent a shudder through her and made the drums in her head pound faster and harder.

She tried again. 'What about—?'

'The group voted unanimously in favor of you,' Alice

said firmly. 'I'm officially placing the responsibility of his gift on your shoulders. If he doesn't have something under the tree for our Christmas party...'

She didn't finish her sentence, but her meaning was obvious. Dr Travers had better have a present by December 19th, or else Lisa's head would roll.

'What are you getting the others?' she asked, wondering if she could discover the brand of cologne he preferred.

'We're paying one day's green fees for Drs Benington and Foster at the Lakewood Country Club. Dr Provo is getting two season passes to the Community Theatre and we're going to purchase Super Bowl tickets for Dr Henry. Which leaves Dr Travers. I'll be honest—after an hour of discussion, we were stumped.'

So much for her cologne idea. A bottle of fragrance didn't compare to a chance to attend the Super Bowl.

Alice rose and patted Lisa on the shoulder. 'I'm sure you'll find something appropriate. Just let me know your idea as soon as you can. By the way, gift certificates are out. Too impersonal.'

Alice left, the faint scent of her perfume hanging in the air as the only sign of her presence.

Lisa rubbed her temples at the thought of the daunting task ahead of her. Still, it couldn't be too hard, she reasoned. After all, everyone had a hobby of some sort. If she put her mind to it, she could surely stumble across a useful piece of information.

As close-mouthed as he was, she'd have to be creative. Unfortunately, with her head pounding in time to her heartbeat, creativity was in short supply at the moment.

Noting the time, Lisa gathered up her charts and returned them to SueEllen's office for filing. The receptionist handed her several sheets of paper.

'These just came over the fax,' she announced. 'Would you mind giving them to Dr Travers?'

'No problem.'

'Oh, and Mrs Rajewski is here for her appointment.'

'I'll be right with her.' Lisa headed for Simon's office, hoping he hadn't returned from lunch so she could snoop. At this rate, she'd earn her magic decoder ring before Christmas.

The door was open, the room empty. She placed the papers on his desk and systematically studied the surface. A series of stackable trays on the left-hand side held medical journals, newsletters, pharmaceutical information and incoming mail. On the right, a pile of patient files waited for his attention.

A plain pencil cup held several pens bearing the names of drugs recently peddled by pharmaceutical reps and a cheap letter-opener. A quartz paperweight sat on a pile of pink telephone messages. No clues there.

Diplomas and a framed poster of a white-sanded beach with an ocean liner in the distance hung on the wall. Several mugs screenprinted with pharmaceutical logos joined the medical books on his shelves. She'd expected to see photos of his sister or his niece and nephew, but didn't find a snapshot or any other personal touch.

Discouraged by her failure, she pinched the bridge of her nose to relieve the tension.

'Looking for something?'

Simon's voice brought on an instant feeling of guilt. 'N-no,' she stammered at the sight of him filling the doorway. 'I just brought in some lab results. They're on your desk.'

'Thanks.'

'I'll be going now,' she said inanely. 'Our first patient for the afternoon is here.'

'OK,' he said in his usual mild manner, before he advanced to review the papers in question. 'Let me know when you're ready.'

'I will.' Lisa headed for the door but before she reached the threshold he stopped her with one word.

'Headache?'

She didn't think that he'd noticed. 'Yes.'

His gaze was piercing. 'Have you taken anything for it?'

'Not yet.'

'Let me know if the pain doesn't let up. I might be able to help.'

At a loss for words, she simply nodded before she escaped. She couldn't imagine what he could do for her. Acetaminophen would have to suffice until she got home and could take something stronger.

After swallowing a few tablets, she called for Mrs Rajewski. 'What's the weather like?' she asked the forty-eight-year-old salt-and-pepper-haired woman as she ushered her to the scales and recorded her weight.

'It's warmed up since this morning,' Mrs Rajewski said with a tired smile.

Seconds later, Lisa shepherded her into an exam room. 'What can we do for you today?' she asked, taking her blood pressure.

'It's time for my annual physical,' Mrs Rajewski said. 'Past time, in fact. I've put it off for a few months, but these last few weeks I've been so tired I can hardly function. I thought I'd better come in.'

'Good idea.' Lisa recorded the numbers, then retrieved a paper sheet and disposable gown from the cupboard, before setting out the speculum and Pap-smear collection kit. 'You know the routine. Doctor and I will be back in a few minutes.'

She left the room and went in search of Simon. He was

still in his office, standing at the window and staring outside with a brooding expression on his face.

'We're ready for you,' she announced, wondering at the direction his thoughts had taken to make him appear so intense.

'I'm coming.'

He followed her down the hall. 'Headache better?' he asked.

She shrugged. 'I'll live.'

'That's not what I asked,' he chided gently. Once again she heard the subtle amusement in his tone.

'I'm OK. Honest.'

Simon arched his eyebrow in disbelief, but they had reached his patient's room and the subject was dropped. Lisa experienced the most sneaking suspicion that her reprieve was only temporary.

'Hello, Mrs Rajewski,' he said on entering. 'It's too nice a day to be stuck in a doctor's office, isn't it?'

Their patient was sitting on the edge of the table, wearing her gown with the sheet covering her lap. 'Absolutely,' she agreed.

Lisa moved to the other side of the table, ready to assist him and lend Mrs Rajewski any moral support.

'Any problems?' he asked as he listened to her heart and lungs. 'Take a deep breath, please.'

Mrs Rajewski complied. 'No more than usual,' she said when she caught her breath again. 'Although I'm more tired than ever and I've noticed several small knots in my right breast. I've been told about having cysts, but these seem larger than before.'

'Do you regularly check yourself?' he asked.

'Every month.'

'Excellent. In any case, we'll take a close look,' he assured her.

Lisa helped her lie on the table before Simon began the exam. 'It's hard to believe that November is half over,' he commented, obviously trying to place his patient at ease.

'Time just flies,' the woman agreed. 'It won't be long and it will be Christmas. Just thinking of all the fuss involved makes me want to skip the month of December and go right into January.'

'I've heard lots of people say that,' Simon said. His fingers stilled, then palpated for the edge of the lump he'd discovered. 'Is this what you were referring to?'

'Yes.'

'She had a mammogram last year,' Lisa offered.

'Good. That will be helpful.' He moved on to Mrs Rajewski's left side, picking up the thread of the conversation as if it had never been dropped. 'So you're one of those people who run themselves ragged during the holidays?'

'I don't intend to,' Mrs Rajewski admitted. 'It sort of happens. I just dread buying gifts. It's so hard to know what people will like.'

'I have the same problem,' Lisa broke into the conversation, thinking of the task she'd been assigned.

'It's the thought that counts,' Simon reminded them.

'True,' Lisa said with a smile, 'but it's nice to get something you can actually use, or want. I always worry over what to buy the men on my list.'

Lisa was surprised at how swiftly Simon's head came up to meet her gaze. A question appeared in his eyes, but before she could guess what it was he looked away. 'We're not so hard to please,' he protested. 'Women are much more difficult.'

Mrs Rajewski rolled her eyes at Lisa. 'Is that why we always get stuck with kitchen appliances? Have you ever wondered how many men find a blender or a bread machine under the tree with their name on it?'

Simon laughed and the deep rich tone caused a smile to cross Lisa's face. He didn't laugh often, at least not in her presence, and she always thought it sounded somewhat rusty from disuse.

He motioned to Lisa that he was ready to begin the pelvic exam, so she helped the older woman move into position. Moments later he was finished and Lisa had sprayed the cell fixative on the slides.

'I used to stew over what I'd give my Fred,' Mrs Rajewski admitted after Simon had stripped off his gloves and was washing his hands. 'Then I discovered the perfect gift.'

'Really?' Lisa couldn't wait to hear. Mrs Rajewski probably had a lot of ideas.

'Well,' the woman began, 'he always needs work clothes, so the kids and I buy jeans, flannel shirts, socks, underwear—the works.'

Lisa groaned at the mental picture of Simon opening a box in front of the entire staff to find shirts, socks and underwear. She forced herself to keep the disappointment out of her voice. 'How nice.'

'But that's not all,' Mrs Rajewski continued, her eyes twinkling. 'Since the kids are teenagers now and can stay by themselves for a few days, I make reservations for the two of us at a fancy hotel.' She smiled and her face turned pink. 'If we've had a good year, crop-wise, I book the honeymoon suite.'

Unbidden, Lisa's gaze fell on Simon at the same moment that he glanced at her. Once again her imagination took over and she couldn't stop the warmth that spread across her face. In fact, her entire body temperature seemed to rise several degrees.

Simon's mouth curved into a slow smile. 'What a unique present.' His gaze remained fixed on her and the gleam in his eyes became so intense that it took a great force of will on her part to break contact.

Mrs Rajewski blithely continued on, clearly oblivious to the sparks shooting between her doctor and his nurse. 'Gives us both something to look forward to. After nearly twenty years of marriage, we need all the spice we can get.'

She patted Lisa's hand. 'Now, don't you forget my gift-giving idea. It may come in handy some day.'

Lisa avoided meeting Simon's gaze, certain he would read her wayward thoughts. 'I won't,' she promised, hoping her face hadn't turned from pink to red.

To her relief, Simon steered the conversation back to a professional footing. 'I'm going to order a few blood tests because anemia could be the cause of your exhaustion. I see in the past notes that Dr Unruh discussed the possibility of a hysterectomy.'

'I've been putting it off,' she admitted. 'Just when I think I'll have the surgery, my periods aren't as heavy and I decide to wait.'

'If you are, indeed, anemic then we can't postpone it much longer,' he told her. 'Lisa will draw a blood sample. Once I receive the results, I may refer you to Dr Henry for a GYN consult.'

'OK.'

He scribbled the procedures he wanted—a CBC, general chemistry and thyroid panel, and an iron level—and handed the chart to Lisa.

'And the lumps?' Traces of fear were in Mrs Rajewski's voice.

'We'll know more after we run another mammogram. As soon as we have all those reports, we'll decide what to do next. In the meantime, don't worry,' he said kindly, placing a hand on her shoulder before he left.

Lisa listened to Mrs Rajewski's chatter with half an ear as she drew the necessary tubes of blood. After she was through, she sent her to SueEllen who arranged for her mammogram at the local hospital.

Thanks to being booked solid with patients all afternoon, her dream of leaving early never materialized. At odd moments she noticed Simon studying her, but she pasted a huge smile on her face and trudged on with her duties.

As soon as the last patient left at five o'clock, she hurriedly straightened the room, pushing herself to finish in record time. Satisfied with her efforts, she turned to leave and found Simon leaning comfortably against the doorframe. He looked as if he'd been there for some time.

He straightened. 'Knowing your sleuthing abilities, I was afraid you'd pull another Carmen San Diego act before I could catch you.'

'Did you need something?'

He advanced within arm's reach. 'I don't, but you do.'

She stared at him, puzzled. Her headache was making her thoughts run slowly. 'What do I need?'

He smiled. 'My services.'

CHAPTER TWO

'YOUR services?' Lisa said.

Her wide eyes and the way she said 'services' made Simon wonder exactly what she thought he was offering. Flattered by the idea of her mind wandering in such an intimate direction where he was concerned, he suppressed a smile before he elaborated.

'My medical expertise. You have the honor of being my last patient for the day.'

'You don't need to bother,' she began.

'Oh, but I do. I can't have my nurse operating at less than peak efficiency again tomorrow.'

She visibly bristled. 'I wasn't aware you had a problem with my work this afternoon.'

He grinned at her reaction. She was conscientious to a fault and clearly didn't take slurs kindly. 'I'm not complaining, but you have to confess to struggling at times. You also weren't as chipper as you usually are.'

A mulish expression came to her face as she nibbled on her bottom lip. However, she didn't argue, so she obviously recognized the truth in his comment. 'I'm fine,' she muttered.

Simon tipped her chin up with his index finger. 'I'm a doctor, remember? I can see those shadows under your eyes, the pinched lines around your mouth. You're in pain and you're too stubborn to admit it.'

'All right. I have an excruciating, eye-popping, my-skull's-going-to-explode headache. Happy?'

'If you're in such pain, why didn't you say something?'

She shrugged. 'Why complain? The help I need is at home. In my medicine cabinet. Needless to say, I couldn't leave you alone to deal with these patients—you'd have been here until midnight.'

'I'd have managed. If not, I could have pulled a nurse from one of the larger practices.'

'I didn't want to bother you,' she muttered, avoiding his gaze. 'You've already heard enough whining patients today. You don't need me to round out your quota.'

He addressed her arguments one by one. 'I offered. You wouldn't have been whining and you're not bothering me in the slightest. Unless you're going to be difficult.'

Her eyes narrowed. 'No offense, but what can you do for me?'

'I'm going to make the pain go away.'

'Aren't you being a *little* over-confident?'

'No,' he said honestly. 'I've dealt with tension headaches before. With extraordinary success, I might add.'

'I've been to more specialists than I can count. The best they can do is prescribe a pill that knocks me out for hours.'

'In that case, you won't mind if I try?' He raised one eyebrow, waiting for her permission.

She heaved an exasperated sigh. 'Oh, all right,' she said crossly. 'You can't do any worse than the others.'

Without giving her time to change her mind, he grabbed her by the shoulders and turned her so that she stood with her back in front of him.

He placed his fingers on her temples and rubbed, inhaling the springtime scent on her short, light brown hair. Next, he skimmed his fingers across her forehead, above her eyebrows, and along her cheekbones.

'Is this where it hurts?'

'Actually, it's all over my head,' she murmured, 'but the pain started there.'

'OK.' Abruptly he moved to her side, placed the palm of his left hand against her forehead and slipped his right hand through her hair to find the base of her skull. For a few seconds he simply rubbed small circles with his thumb and index finger, noticing how her hair felt like corn silk against the back of his hand.

'What are you doing?' she asked, the tension in her voice fading as the stiff set to her shoulders eased.

Simon continued to massage the back of her head. 'This may hurt.' Without giving further warning, he pressed the two points at the base of her skull, holding her head between his hands.

She yelped and tried to break free, but he held her in his vise-like grip. 'Hang on as long as you can,' he told her. 'Relax.'

Lisa squirmed. 'Relax? How can I when you're trying to make my head explode?' Her arms flailed until her left hand brushed against his chest. Immediately, she latched onto the front of his shirt and twisted the fabric into a tight knot. The discomfort he experienced at having his chest hair pulled was minor when compared to the pain she was most likely experiencing, and to compensate he concentrated on the feel of her fingers resting against his solar plexus.

It was as if she'd branded him with her touch, and the idea made it difficult to remember that theirs was only a professional relationship.

Even with that reminder, he struggled to begin counting. As soon as he reached ten he eased the pressure and gradually began pushing downward along the muscles in her neck.

She sighed and her fingers relaxed against his chest. Without warning, he repeated the process.

Once again she twisted his shirt and he felt the cotton

fabric inch out of his waistband. Yet he couldn't do a thing about it, except hope that no one would chance by the open door. He could imagine the chagrin on her face if she realized what she was doing.

Neither did it take a lot of speculation on his part to guess at the ribbing she'd get from the rest of the staff if they were discovered in what some might have called a compromising situation.

Simon released the pressure and repeated the entire process a third time. A quick glance down at himself made him smile. His shirt was almost totally untucked.

'How's the head?' he asked.

She hesitated, obviously taking stock. 'Better.'

He went through the routine twice more, noticing that Lisa's hold on his shirt didn't slacken, even when he eased the pressure. Finally she sagged, as if her knees couldn't hold her any more, and he knew it was time to stop.

Yet he couldn't. He didn't want the experience of having her this close, resting in his embrace, to end.

He *refused* to let it end. The only thought on his mind was to savour the moment and prolong it as long as decently possible.

Simon pulled her back against him and felt a sense of masculine pride stir in his chest over her reluctance to release his shirt.

He tipped her face up until her head rested underneath his chin. Immediately, he began massaging her forehead, temples and cheekbones.

Her whole body relaxed against him. He didn't mind. From their first day together, he'd felt a remarkable sense of peace in her presence. She wasn't prone to idle chatter and respected his privacy—rare traits in the women he knew. During his weak moments he'd allowed himself to play the game of 'what if', although he knew nothing could come of it.

At least, not now. Maybe after the choppy waters of his life had smoothed out and he was sailing on an even keel, he could do something about his attraction to her. The burden that had been thrust upon him fifteen years ago suddenly felt more restrictive than usual.

But even without those familial responsibilities weighing him down, he couldn't indulge himself with this woman. Not only was she his subordinate, a colleague, but she deserved a more intimate setting for a stolen kiss than a busy medical office. Although few staff members ventured into their wing, he wouldn't take the chance.

He ran his fingers along the bridge of her nose, noticing a small cluster of freckles sprinkled across her skin. To be honest, he enjoyed looking at her and intended to enjoy this opportunity to feast his eyes.

Her bone structure was good, her features perfect. Others might think her mouth too wide, her nose too long and narrow, but to him she was beautiful.

Her loose, pale blue scrub suit hung on a slender but well-shaped figure. Her fingers were long and delicate, but he'd seen their strength as she'd tussled with a belligerent child, their gentleness as she'd cuddled a baby or assisted a geriatric patient.

Lisa was everything he could possibly want in a woman.

Right now, she stood out of reach.

A telephone rang in the distance. The chances of discovery increased with each passing moment. Simon stilled his hands and cleared his throat.

'How's the headache?' He winced at hearing his brusque tone.

She opened her eyes and lifted her head off his chest.

For a long moment she didn't answer, as if trying to decide. 'Why, it's gone.'

He grinned. 'What did I tell you?'

She touched her forehead. 'I can't believe it. The pain is one hundred per cent better. Where did you learn that technique?'

'From a chiropractor friend of mine,' he said modestly. 'It's come in handy a time or two.'

'Too bad more people don't know your trick. It beats being dopey for hours. Now I know who to go to when I get a headache.'

'My hands are available any time.' As soon as he spoke he realized his unintentional *double entendre* and wondered if she had, too. From the look of amazed awe lingering on her face, he doubted it.

'Aren't you glad you let me work my magic?'

Her smile was as brilliant as a ray of July sunshine. 'Magic is right. I can't believe the improvement. For a while there, I thought you were going to crush my head into a million pieces. I didn't mean to grab onto you, but—'

Her horrified gasp and her wide eyes made him take stock of his appearance. If one of his partners saw him right now, he'd have some explaining to do.

Immediately he smoothed away the wrinkles, wondered if he'd find his missing button and began tucking his shirt tails into his trousers.

Her hands flew to her face. 'Oh, my. I can't believe I...I ripped...pulled... Oh, dear.'

He grinned. 'You did react more strongly than most.'

'I'm *so* sorry,' she apologized. 'You can't imagine how sorry I am.'

'It's OK, Lisa,' he soothed as he finished making himself presentable. 'I didn't mind.' Not one bit.

'You must think I'm—'

'You were in pain and didn't know what you were doing. Don't worry about it.'

She smoothed at the wrinkles. 'I'll fix your shirt for you,' she said, her voice rushed and breathless. 'It's the least I can do for you.'

The combination of her touch and his thoughts created an unholy response. Immediately, he grabbed her wrists before things flew completely out of hand. 'It isn't necessary. The folks at the dry-cleaners do minor repairs.'

She tugged on the gold chain around her neck. 'Are you sure?' she asked, her uncertainty showing in her eyes.

He smiled, forcing himself not to gaze at her mouth like a lovesick schoolboy who was anxious for a kiss and too shy to act. 'I'm positive.'

'Aren't you ready to go yet, Lisa?' Savanna asked from the doorway, her curiosity plain as she took in the scene. 'I thought you were in a hurry to get a ride home.'

Simon was amused by the speed at which Lisa jumped in front of him, as if to shield his appearance from her friend. 'I was, but I don't need a ride after all.'

Savanna blinked in surprise. 'I thought you had a headache.'

'I did, but I don't now. Simon, er, Dr Travers made it go away. Reflexology, I guess.' She glanced at him for confirmation, before adding, 'I can drive myself home.'

'Wow, you must be good,' Savanna said, obviously awed.

'Adequate,' Simon responded with a small smile. Sensing that a retreat was in order before the other nurse raised unanswerable questions, he added, 'See you ladies tomorrow. Have a nice evening.'

'You, too.' Lisa hurried through the door, grabbing Savanna's arm and pulling her along.

'What's the rush?'

'Just listen,' Lisa instructed, letting go of her friend. 'Go straight to my house. I have to talk.'

Savanna halted in her tracks. 'What happened in there?'

'I'll tell you when you get to my house,' Lisa said.

'Why do I feel like I'm on a top secret mission?' Savanna grumbled, although her eyes gleamed with interest.

Lisa pushed her toward the door. 'Just go. I'll be right behind you.'

During the drive to her apartment building, the whole incident replayed itself in Lisa's mind. How could she face Simon again? She'd ruined everything. She'd never be able to work next to him without remembering how good it had felt to lean on him, to wrap her hands in his shirt, to feel his chest underneath her hands.

'I'm going to have to quit,' she announced to Savanna a short time later as she cleared the table of piano books and waited for the kettle to boil.

Savanna made herself at home and found two mugs. 'Does this have something to do with you trying to rip Dr Travers's clothes off his gorgeous body?'

Lisa's jaw dropped. 'How did you know?'

Savanna grinned an evil grin. 'A wild guess.'

Lisa groaned and buried her face in her hands.

'I caught a glimpse of his shirt. Even on a bad day, with hordes of screaming, snot-nosed kids, he always looks like he stepped off a magazine cover. I knew you were hiding something the moment you jumped in front of him. I added two and two together and came up with four.'

'He was doing this thing with my head—'

'Yeah, right.'

'You can just wipe that smirk off your face,' Lisa said tartly as she straightened. 'He was. My head hurt so bad, and when he started squeezing my skull my knees went weak. I grabbed him to keep my balance.'

'Sure you did.'

'It's true.'

Savanna wriggled her eyebrows. 'Be glad you only tore off a shirt button. You could have broken worse things, like his belt.'

'Will you be serious?' Lisa scolded, shuddering at the image Savanna had planted in her brain. 'Anyway, when it was all over, I saw what I'd done. How can I ever face him again?'

Deep in her misery, Lisa didn't notice that the kettle had started to whistle or that Savanna had helped herself until her friend shoved a steaming cup of water under her nose.

'I don't know what you're worried about,' Savanna said, spooning coffee granules into their cups. 'He didn't act upset to have your hands running all over him.'

'They weren't all over him. Just over his chest,' she corrected weakly. 'What am I going to do?'

Savanna leaned forward, her blue eyes intent. 'There's nothing to do.'

'How can you say that?'

'It was just something that happened, a fluke. You can either go to work tomorrow, crawl back in your usual aloof shell and hold him at arm's length like you have ever since he came on board, or you can loosen up, consider the formal ice between you two broken and let the interest you have in him blossom.'

'I don't hold him at arm's length,' Lisa protested. 'As for my interest, who said I had any in Dr Travers?' she finished on a defiant note.

Savanna rolled her eyes. 'If you didn't, you wouldn't be worried about what he'd think. Be honest. If this had happened with Roger, or anyone else for that matter, you'd be laughing and wouldn't give the matter a second thought.'

Lisa drew in a tremulous breath. Savanna was right. Dr Travers was the stuff of dreams, but she'd seen too many office romances turn sour. She didn't intend to fall into that trap. Life was difficult enough when a courtship involving the boy next door ended.

'I can't very well flirt with him. It would ruin our working relationship.'

'Maybe. Maybe not.'

Lisa ignored the carrot named hope dangling before her eyes. 'As for me crawling into my usual "aloof" shell, I'll have you know that I have lots of male friends.'

'Sure you do. You treat every one of them like you'd treat a cousin or a big brother.'

'Because I don't feel any of those special sparks. I'm not interested in flirting with everyone who comes along.'

Savanna gave an unladylike snort. 'I don't mean *everyone*. I'm talking about an occasional fellow. Surely someone's caught your eye in the last twelve months.'

Lisa leaned back and crossed her arms. 'I've noticed lots of attractive men. They just haven't been…' She paused. 'My type.'

'I don't know how you'll figure out what your type is if you don't go out with anyone. Just so you'll know, I'm making it my personal goal to scout out and introduce you to a few handsome hunks while we're sailing to Nassau.'

Seeing the twinkle in her friend's eyes, Lisa groaned. Savanna's boldness knew no bounds and Lisa could already imagine the shipboard events planned to thrust her into male company.

Savanna planted her elbows on the table and leaned forward. 'Forget about our vacation right now. Dr Travers seems to be a great guy. If you ask me, you're passing up a golden opportunity, not only to expand your romantic horizons but to find out whatever you can about him. Need I remind you? You *are* responsible for his Christmas gift.'

'Speaking of which,' Lisa said, ready to vent her feelings on that subject as well, 'what's the deal about you and

Roger voting me for the job? You know how I feel about Christmas.'

Savanna shrugged. 'You can't hate the holiday for ever. Now is as good a time as any to regain your Christmas cheer.'

'Have you been talking to my mother again?'

'She's only worried about you. As for Roger, he simply pointed out how you spend the most time with Dr Travers and I agreed. The rest, as they say, is history.'

'Gee, thanks. Roger's turn is coming.'

'Don't be so hard on him. He was just jealous of you for being more sneaky than he was. How *did* you get away?'

Lisa pretended horror. 'Divulge my escape plan? Not a chance. I may need it again.'

'Speaking of plans, do you have one to figure out what to buy Dr Travers?'

'Not really. I thought I'd start by asking leading questions, but if I have to find a different job because Simon thinks I'm intruding on his private life, I'll know who to blame.'

Savanna waved her hands in carefree abandon. 'You're not asking for his deepest, darkest secrets, only his likes and dislikes. It'll all work out. Trust me. And who knows? You may thank me someday.'

'Fat chance.'

The next morning, as Lisa braced herself to meet Simon, the only thing she could thank her friend for was her sleepless night.

She'd worn her newest scrub suit, teal green pants with a co-ordinating multicolored top in a swirling design that just happened to match the tropical storm in her stomach.

You can face him. Those four words echoed in her mind as she left the lounge with a peace offering in her hand and headed for the building's far right wing where Simon's small suite of offices was housed. She'd have preferred to have hidden, but calling in sick was cowardly. It only postponed the inevitable. Considering how he'd been concerned over her headache, he might call her at home or, worse yet, drop by.

Her best plan was to act normally, or as normally as possible, considering her Christmas assignment. He would never guess how for those private moments under his ministrations the reality of tearing at his clothes had edged close to her fantasy.

Lisa placed the plate of cookies on his desk, along with Mrs Rajewski's faxed lab report. If she was truly brave, she'd search his office in depth before he arrived, but, to her, rummaging through the desk drawers for personal effects was the height of an invasion of privacy. Also, her nerves wouldn't stand the strain of being caught redhanded. Receiving answers to pointed questions was her best and least stressful option.

Before temptation could coax her into compromising her principles, she turned sharply on one heel and disappeared into their small lab.

She found a box of decorations on one countertop, strategically placed so as not to be missed. Recognizing Alice's not-so-subtle hint to get in the Christmas spirit like every other office, Lisa began rummaging through its contents.

The rest of the clinic had foregone the Thanksgiving motif and had already hung their fake holly, evergreen wreaths and tinsel. Considering that she wasn't thrilled with reminders of the holiday, she decided to decorate with the philosophy of 'less was more'.

Intent on choosing several holiday pictures to thumbtack on the bulletin board and adorn the exam-room doors, she didn't notice Simon's soundless approach until he stood close enough for her to breathe in his special scent.

For a split second she tensed, but his easy grin as he

peered over her shoulder to focus on the colorful paper Christmas tree made her relax.

'Couldn't hold out against the pressure, huh?'

Granted, the clock hadn't even turned to nine a.m., but it wasn't fair for him to look as if he'd stepped out of a storefront display. His black trousers had razor-sharp creases, and the collar points of his dark green shirt were as perfect as the knot in his matching tie. Not a single hair hung out of place, although she knew it was a windy morning and could hear an occasional gust sweep against the building.

She grinned. 'Yeah, I decided to go with the flow. But I'm not going to get carried away, like some people in the building.'

'Good idea. How's the head?'

His abrupt change in topic brought her a split second's unease, but she heard only curiosity in his voice.

'Never better.'

'No after-effects?'

Only a remarkable awareness of you. Adding yesterday's incident to the sparks she'd attributed to static electricity, she was in terrible trouble. Because her reaction was horribly one-sided, Simon must never know how she truly felt.

'None.'

'Good.'

Determined to begin her own agenda, she asked, 'How was your evening?'

'Fine.'

'Did you do anything special?'

He shook his head. 'Did you?'

'Not really. I baked sugar cookies. By the way, I left a plate in your office in case you couldn't make it to the lounge before those all disappeared.'

'Thanks.'

He turned to leave. She quickly tried to continue their conversation. 'Do you like sugar cookies?'

'Yes.'

'I didn't know if you preferred chocolate chip, or peanut butter, or oatmeal raisin, or—' Land sakes! She was babbling.

'I'm happy with anything.'

If she hadn't been a mature twenty-seven-year-old, she would have stomped her foot in childish frustration. 'What's your *favorite*?'

'Anything fresh out of the oven. Did we get Mrs Rajewski's lab results yet?'

She wasn't surprised by his return to professional topics, although she was disappointed by his reticence over something as basic and non-threatening as food. At this rate, she might learn his favorite TV program by Christmas.

'I've already laid them on your desk.'

'Good.'

Simon disappeared into his office while Lisa finished choosing her decorations, aggrieved by her failure to discover his preferred type of cookie. Finding an appropriate gift would be no easy task.

She could always gift-wrap a barrel of home-made goodies, she supposed. Or sign him up for the Cookie-of-the-Month Club. Sadly, home-made treats—no matter how good—didn't fall into the same league as Super Bowl football tickets. He deserved something special, too.

She desperately needed a hint, an idea, or a suggestion of some sort…

CHAPTER THREE

SIMON met her in the hallway, holding a white page in one hand and a cookie in the other. 'I just read Lorna Rajewski's lab results. Did you?'

'Sorry,' Lisa confessed. 'I only glanced at them. Did you find something wrong?'

'Her hemoglobin is under eight grams. No wonder the woman's tired.'

'Normal's around twelve, isn't it?'

'Yeah. She can't put off her hysterectomy any longer. Her abnormal bleeding is affecting her entire body and I'd rather deal with it before we have a crisis situation.'

'Sounds like we're not far off.'

'No, we're not. Which is why I want you to call Henry and set up an appointment for her as soon as possible.'

'I'll get right on it.'

'Any word on her mammogram?'

'I couldn't get her in until Friday morning. They'll fax the results.'

He pressed his mouth into a line. 'If that's the best we can do, then we'll have to wait. Let me know when Henry will see her and I'll call her at home.'

'Will do.'

Lisa dialed the OB-GYN office extension and requested an appointment. After his receptionist gave her a date, Lisa strode into Simon's office and handed him the scrap of paper. 'Next Monday. Three p.m.'

Simon studied her note. 'This phone number. Who's—?'

'It's Mrs Rajewski's.' Lisa had anticipated the need and jotted it down.

'Thanks.'

Lisa noticed that the plate of cookies no longer rested on his desk. A surreptitious glance found the goodies on top of the filing cabinet in the far corner of the room.

He didn't like them after all.

Her dismal thought must have showed on her face. 'I had to move them,' he commented in an offhand manner.

'What?'

He motioned in the direction of his filing cabinet. 'I had to move them. They're much too tempting and I'm trying to restrain myself so they'll last longer.'

His compliment created a warm glow inside her. 'I'm glad you think so, but there's more where they came from.'

He patted his flat stomach. 'A comforting thought, but I don't dare. Each one is probably worth an hour of exercise time.'

Lisa immediately pictured him in athletic shorts and a tight-fitting T-shirt, lifting weights or running along a track. His muscles would move like those of a sleek racehorse as a sheen of perspiration covered his skin.

'I forgot to tell you. I left all the calories at my house,' she teased. 'You're safe.'

He grinned. 'You've just convinced me to have another one.' He rose to help himself.

'So do you belong to the health club?' Maybe they could buy a treadmill or a stair-stepper machine.

'Yes, but I rarely go. I usually use my neighbor's indoor pool.'

Her imagination didn't have to stretch far to see him in swimming trunks, his hair plastered against his head with water streaming off his body as he completed his laps.

Considering his washboard stomach and muscular torso, he faithfully followed an exercise regimen.

She suppressed a sigh. They certainly didn't share a love for water. She couldn't swim a single stroke, which was why she planned to stay within grabbing distance of her life-jacket during her cruise.

Her impulsive idea to invest in fitness equipment slipped down the drain. 'I'd better see if our first patient has arrived,' she muttered, escaping to the common reception area.

'Hey, Lisa.' SueEllen, their receptionist, who'd celebrated her twenty-ninth birthday for the fourth time, greeted her at the window with a patient folder. 'It's too early to wear such a frown. What's wrong?'

'I'm coming up blank with Christmas ideas for Dr Travers,' she admitted.

SueEllen gave her a sympathetic glance. 'I'm sure you'll think of something.'

'I hope so.' Lisa recognized the name on the file. She opened the door to the waiting area and called for Holly Brooks.

Moments later, the entire Brooks family, including the mother Yvonne, five-year-old daughter Andrea and eighteen-month-old Troy followed Lisa to an exam room.

'I'm sorry I had to bring everyone,' Yvonne apologized. 'But I didn't have a sitter.'

'Not a problem,' Lisa said cheerfully, noticing how Andrea took Troy to one corner and sat down to play with him while Yvonne held Holly on her lap. All the children resembled their mother, both in their facial features and dark coloring.

Holly's face was flushed, her eyes dull, her expression tearful—definite signs of a sick child, and ones that Lisa had seen often in this particular patient over the past year.

'What's Holly's problem today?' she asked, using the ear thermometer to take her temperature.

'Sore throat, as usual. I suppose it's tonsillitis, again.' Yvonne's voice sounded weary and her own demeanor reflected defeat.

A beep signaled the end of the wait and Lisa read the digital display. One hundred and two degrees Fahrenheit. 'Holly has a temperature,' she remarked, recording the number on her nursing notes. 'I'll fetch Doctor and be right back.'

Lisa found Simon in the lab. 'Your first patient is ready. Looks like it's going to be another busy day.'

She hurried away to call for the next patient, and placed forty-five-year-old Kenneth Wright in the room next to Holly's. 'What can we help you with?' she asked.

A glimmer of perspiration appeared above Ken's upper lip. 'I'm in terrible pain. Back here.' He pointed to his kidneys. 'My urine is really dark.'

'Have you ever been diagnosed with a kidney stone?' she asked.

He shook his head.

'Do you drink lots of water?'

'Some. Not as much as I probably should.'

Lisa took his temperature, counted his pulse rate, then strapped on the blood-pressure cuff. 'As soon as I'm finished, I'll send you to the rest room for a urine sample.' After she'd recorded her figures—all of them within normal limits—she pointed him in the direction of the toilet.

'The cups are in there. Just leave your specimen in the little window and I'll pick it up later.'

Ken nodded his agreement, his face pale under his tan as he slowly walked away.

Lisa washed her hands, then hurried back to the

Brookses' room. She arrived just in time to hear Simon's diagnosis above Holly's weak cries.

'Those tonsils have to come out,' he said. 'According to her records, Holly has suffered with this problem repeatedly over the past year.'

Yvonne bit her lip. 'I know.'

Lisa knew the reason behind Mrs Brooks's hesitation. As a single parent, she struggled on her income as a waitress. Although she had health insurance, her particular policy had a high deductible, which meant that she had a large out-of-pocket expense before the insurance company picked up the balance. To Lisa's knowledge, Mr Brooks was completely out of the picture and she doubted strongly if he paid any child support.

She met Simon's gaze and knew from his expression that they were thinking alike. 'You can't put this off much longer,' he said gently.

Yvonne stroked her daughter's hair, before running her fingertips along her hot little face. The child quieted, resting her head against her mother's chest. Her sobs turned to sniffles. 'OK. What do we have to do?'

'First, Lisa will swab Holly's throat for a culture. I'll start her on antibiotics. In the meantime, I'm calling our ear, nose and throat specialist to let him know that you've decided to act on his earlier recommendation.'

'And then?'

'And then, when her infection clears up, Dr Howard will schedule her surgery. Children usually bounce back from this procedure quickly. He'll explain everything in more detail when he sees you. As for today, I'll give you some antibiotic samples to use.'

Simon left Lisa to follow his orders. After much coaxing and some difficulty in getting Holly to open her mouth again so she could swab her throat, Lisa collected her specimens.

'We'll have the report in forty-eight hours so, unless something unusual shows up in the culture, she should improve with the medicine I'll give you,' Lisa said. 'If not, call us.'

'I will.'

Lisa dispensed the samples Simon had directed and sent the family on their way. She left Holly's throat swabs in their small med room for the courier to transport to the Farmington Hospital lab, then tested Ken Wright's urine specimen.

Because the fluid was red-tinged, rather than a normal pale yellow color, she wasn't surprised to find that the chemical test strip showed large amounts of blood. Although a UTI sometimes brought on these same symptoms, she didn't detect any trace of white blood cells. Moving a kidney stone to her list of possible causes, she recorded the results on a small form and went in search of Simon.

Rounding the corner, she ran into Matt Holden, a twelve-year-old who had weekly allergy injections, and his mother, Tricia.

'Is it four o'clock already?' she asked, surprised to see him.

Matt's grin revealed the wire retainer on his teeth. He was dark-headed, shorter than most boys his age and always wore an impish smile. His fudge-brown eyes shone with intelligence and an orneriness that reminded Lisa of her brothers.

'Nah. We didn't have school today. Parent-teacher conferences,' he said.

'Your room is empty,' she instructed mother and son. 'I'll be right with you.'

Before they could go their separate ways, Simon came out of Ken's room. 'Hi, Matt,' he said, holding out his hand to exchange a high five with the youngster. 'It must be Tuesday if you're here.'

'That's right,' Matt replied. 'But we don't have school today, so I wanted to get this over with early.'

'Good idea,' Simon answered. He addressed Lisa. 'I want a stat IVP on Mr Wright. Schedule a urology consult, too.'

'Do you think he has a stone?'

'More than likely, but we'll see what shows on the X-ray.'

'Will do,' she said, moving toward the telephone to make the arrangements. After a brief conversation, she'd organized the procedure with the technician.

'Go back to the main entrance and take the elevator downstairs to our radiology department,' she instructed Ken. 'They'll work you in right away.'

'I don't go to the hospital?' he asked, showing his surprise.

'We have our own X-ray department,' she told him. 'It saves time because you don't have to navigate the hospital's red tape or wait as long.'

'That's nice.'

'When you're finished—the procedure takes about an hour—come back to our office and Dr Travers will discuss the findings with you.'

'I will.'

Lisa returned to her med room and drew up Matt's allergy injections in two syringes. She carried her supplies to the 'baby room'—designated as such because it contained specialized equipment for infants and small children—and was pleasantly surprised to find Simon keeping Matt and his mother company.

'Are you ready for me to do the honors?' Lisa asked.

Matt pulled up his sleeve. 'Yeah.'

Lisa disinfected a small area of skin with rubbing alcohol, then injected the first syringe's contents before she repeated the process in his other arm. 'You've come a long way,' she told the boy as she worked. 'Do you remember how we had to practically sit on you to get you to hold still?'

'Screaming murder the entire time,' his mother added.

'You can't be talking about *this* Matt,' Simon joked.

Mrs Holden laughed. 'Definitely this Matt. We postponed allergy shots for years because he'd go crazy if anyone even mentioned the word "needle".'

Matt's face turned ruddy under their gentle teasing. 'I was just a kid. What did you expect?'

Simon chuckled. 'And now you're not, I suppose.'

'No,' Matt insisted. 'I'm more mature and responsible. Which is why Dad said I could have a BB gun for Christmas. I put it on my list.'

'Along with fifteen other things,' his mother said dryly.

Lisa discarded the used syringes into the biohazardous waste containers. She couldn't have planned this any better, she thought, excited at the direction the conversation had taken.

'What else do you want?' she asked as she handed Matt an ice-pack as a precaution against swelling.

'A bigger ten-speed mountain bike,' he said importantly. 'I've outgrown my old one.'

'A BB gun and a bicycle. I'm impressed,' Lisa said.

'But that's not all, is it?' Simon asked, smiling down on the boy.

Matt moved the ice-pack from one arm to the other. 'Nope. I need some new video games. Simon and I have already conquered all the levels on the ones I have.'

Lisa glanced at Simon. 'You play video games?'

He shrugged. 'After I'm through with my swim, I sometimes challenge Matt.'

'He's good, too.' The youngster's praise was sincere.

The intercom system squawked to life. 'Dr Travers. Call on line two.'

Simon straightened. 'Back to work.' He ruffled Matt's short hair as he walked past. 'See you tonight.'

Lisa could hardly wait for him to disappear into his office. 'Do you know Dr Travers well?'

Mrs Holden shrugged. 'In a manner of speaking. He lives next door so we see him quite often when he drops by to use our pool, but he's very close-lipped.'

So these people were his neighbors. What a perfect opportunity. 'What does he do in his spare time?'

'Swims mostly,' Matt said. 'He reads a lot, too. He's really into American history.'

History. Her most dreaded subject. All she could remember was how her teachers had insisted on drilling dates into her head when she would have preferred to study what had made the people tick. Apparently Simon had been fortunate enough to have more interesting teachers than she'd had.

'Why do you want to know?' Mrs Holden asked.

Lisa lowered her voice. 'We're trying to decide on a Christmas gift for him and we've all drawn a blank. I'd appreciate any ideas for something really special.'

'I'm in the same boat,' Mrs Holden confessed. 'Being our neighbour, he looks after our dog when we're out of town, gets our mail, that kind of stuff. We want to repay him, but nothing seems quite right.'

'I know the feeling.'

'If I come across anything appropriate, I'll let you know,' Matt's mother promised.

'Is my time up?' Matt asked, fidgeting in his chair.

Lisa glanced at her watch. He still had a few minutes to go. 'Are you in that big a hurry to leave us?'

He nodded. 'The guys are coming over to shoot some hoops.'

She faked a big sigh. 'I suppose I can cut you some slack today since you have big plans.'

His face brightened. 'Gee, thanks.'

She checked the injection sites for a reaction and found only small, mosquito-bite-sized welts. 'Have fun. See you next week.'

As the two left, Lisa wondered what she could do to find out more about Simon. She could always ask him outright for ideas, but doing so made the holiday seem so commercialized. No, she wanted to surprise him. If she only knew what she could surprise him *with*.

If the worst came to the worst, Lisa would invite him to her family's Thanksgiving dinner. Her mother had wonderful instincts about people and an uncanny ability to make the most closed person drop his guard and confide in her. By the time everyone had stuffed themselves to their ears, Simon Travers's life would be an open book.

On Thursday evening, Lisa roamed through the Farmington Mall in search of her mother's birthday gift. With any luck, she'd lay her eyes on something for Simon, too—something so perfect that his name would be proverbially written on it.

Fat chance, she thought glumly. So far, her efforts to draw him out had been futile. She was becoming too obvious with her questioning, because just that morning Simon had acted puzzled when she'd brought up the subject of Christmas for what was probably the hundredth time that week.

It was time to lie low, before she made him wonder if she had lost her mind.

She sighed. So much for being a master sleuth. She had no choice now but to call her mother for suggestions.

If only she'd bought her mom's birthday present before the merchants had started to promote Christmas with a vengeance. Every display featured seasonal elements, ranging from trees with gaily wrapped packages underneath to figures of Santa Claus.

At the bridal shop she saw mannequins in gorgeous velvet dresses posed around an elaborate cake adorned with holly and red and green satin ribbons.

She hurried past and averted her gaze.

The store next door—Lady-In-Waiting—displayed a variety of maternity wear, infants' and children's clothing in rich, red and hunter-green hues. A Christmas tree at the far end of the display had thousands of baby cartoon characters hanging from the branches.

She stared straight ahead.

The next shop sold every kitchen gadget imaginable and was Lisa's destination. After a consultation with her sister, Jill, and her sister-in-law, Mary, they'd agreed on a bread machine. Lisa had volunteered to find one in their collective price range and, luckily, the model she'd wanted was on sale.

She charged the purchase to her credit card and, after making arrangements for the gift-wrapping, she left the store and planned to return in thirty minutes.

Not in the mood to browse, she headed for the snack bar in the center of the mall. Along the way, a craft and hobby store caught her eye.

She paused outside the plate-glass display window to stare at the huge Scotch pine tree brightly decorated with large maroon satin bows, strands of white pearls, porcelain angels carrying various musical instruments and thousands of clear blinking lights.

Someday, when she was in the mood to celebrate Christmas again, she'd recreate one like it in her own apartment. Granted, it would be on a much smaller scale since she didn't have a spacious living room in her house, but the idea of a musical angel tree appealed to her.

She adjusted the shoulder strap of her bag and sighed. Maybe next year.

'Pretty, isn't it?'

Lisa glanced at Simon, surprised at how easily he could catch her unawares. He'd obviously dropped by right after work just as she had, because under his open trench coat he wore the same clothes as he had earlier in the day.

'Yes.' She motioned to the tree. 'No one should start promoting Christmas until after the first of December. Don't you agree?'

'In theory, yes. But it's the simple economics of supply and demand. People don't like to wait until the last minute, so businessmen bring out their merchandise to catch those early sales.'

'I guess.'

'So, what are you doing out on this blustery evening?' he asked. 'Christmas shopping?'

'Birthday,' she corrected. 'My mother's. How about you?'

'Just looking.'

'For anything in particular?'

'Not really.' For a few seconds he appeared indecisive. 'Mind if I ask you a question?'

'Go ahead.'

'I'm trying to understand why a woman who supposedly doesn't like Christmas has been talking about it constantly this past week.'

Her face warmed. 'I haven't been very subtle, have I?'

Simon smiled. 'You have a way to go before you earn your spy badge.'

She laughed at his comment. 'Don't worry, I won't run away and join the CIA.'

'Good idea. So what gives?'

'I shouldn't tell you this, but every year the clinic staff buys our doctors and PAs a Christmas present. We're— I'm—trying to find out what you'd like.'

'I see.'

'Can you help me out with a few ideas?'

He cocked his head and a wrinkle appeared between his eyes. 'No.'

'No?'

'Not right now,' he corrected. 'I don't know what I want.'

Lordy, he was making this hard. 'I'll rephrase the question. What do you *need*?'

He shrugged. 'I can't think of a thing. I can always use a new tie.'

'Too dull.'

'Lorna Rajewski's suggestion sounded interesting.'

'You want us to book the honeymoon suite for you?' She tried not to show her disappointment over the prospect of a woman in his life. 'I didn't know you had a significant other.'

'I don't. By Christmas, though, who knows?' A dimple appeared in his right cheek. She'd never seen it before and was fascinated by its appearance.

At the same time, relief over his available status surged through her.

'I doubt if our strait-laced Alice would approve of such a present,' she said dryly.

He snapped his fingers. 'Darn. What a shame.'

'Well, if you think of something else, will you let me know?'

'I will,' he promised. In his next breath, he changed the subject. 'So tell me why you don't like Christmas?'

Lisa averted her gaze to stare at the angel tree. 'It's a long story.'

'I've got time.'

'I was on my way for a sandwich and a cup of hot chocolate.'

'I haven't eaten either. Mind if I join you?'

She couldn't think of more enjoyable company or a more enjoyable way to spend a half-hour. 'I'd be delighted.'

He shortened his steps to stride alongside her. 'What did you pick out for your mother?'

'A bread machine. She's always talking about what our neighbour bakes in hers, so my family decided to get her one, too.' In spite of the failed engagement between their children, Rhonda Mallory still remained good friends with Bryan's mother, Polly Lewis, which was one reason why Lisa didn't drop by her childhood home as often. Running into her former future mother-in-law wasn't Lisa's idea of a relaxing visit.

At the snack bar, they placed their orders—hot chocolate and a hamburger for her, black coffee with two sugars and a roast beef sandwich for him.

While they waited for the waitress to call their number, Simon guided her to a private booth near the back of the shop and slid into the seat across the table from her.

'So why don't you like this holiday?' he asked.

'I had my wedding planned for last Christmas. My fiancé, Bryan, and I grew up together. He lived next door and we were always a couple in school. Last November he admitted that he'd fallen in love with someone else.'

'I'm sorry,' he murmured.

She drew a bracing breath. 'What really hurt was that he married her on what should have been *our* wedding day. They used the church *I* had booked, the same caterer, the same florist and color scheme. Other than the dress, it was like she had stepped into *my* wedding.'

'Must have been rough.'

'It wasn't easy,' she agreed, 'but I managed.'

His brows drew together in a thoughtful line. 'Wasn't it better to find out *before* the ceremony that he didn't love you, rather than *after*?'

'Oh, definitely. I'm old-fashioned in that respect. I don't want to wind up as a divorce statistic. It would have been nice, though, if he'd told me about her earlier. Not after I'd already mailed our wedding invitations.'

The memory of her heartache as she'd called everyone on her guest list made the sick feeling in the pit of her stomach return.

'That explains last year. What about this year?'

'Bryan's wife is pregnant and everyone is treating me like spun glass again. Sure, the idea hurts when I think it might have been me, but it's not and I accept that. Unfortunately, because I don't have a social life requiring a secretary, people think I'm withering away like some Victorian maiden.'

'So you're suffering from an overdose of sympathy.'

'Exactly,' she said, pleased that he understood. 'It's like I'm in some Pavlovian experiment and I now associate Christmas carols and trees and presents with everyone patting my hand and reassuring me that the right man will come along. Which is why I asked for my vacation to start on the 22nd. My cruise ship leaves that evening.'

'Going with someone in particular?'

She couldn't tell if he was making idle conversation or

had a specific interest in her companion's identity. 'Savanna Gibson.'

He relaxed. 'Leaving town is one way to deal with your dilemma.'

She raised an eyebrow. 'You don't agree.'

The clerk called their order number and Simon retrieved their tray. After they'd started eating, he picked up the thread of their dropped conversation.

'I can't agree or disagree with your decision,' he said. 'A cruise is nice. I'd love to sail somewhere myself. But when you get back, won't Bryan's wife still be pregnant?'

'It's a temporary solution, I admit, but unless I can whip a boyfriend out of thin air it's the best I can do to show I'm not pining for the man.' She paused, remembering Savanna's initial objections before she'd convinced her. 'Do you think I'm running away, too?'

'It doesn't matter what I think. It's what you think that counts.'

'I refuse to spend another holiday in town listening to people dredge up the past. That chapter of my life is over and I'm ready for something new and exciting. Savanna assures me I'll be too busy to give anyone here at home a second thought.'

'Then I hope you have a wonderful time.'

'Thanks, I will.'

Simon polished off his sandwich and drained the last of his coffee. 'I hate to run, but…'

She glanced at her watch. Her thirty minutes had turned into an hour. 'Me, too. See you in the morning?'

'Bright and early,' he said.

Lisa felt a moment's regret over asking him for his own gift ideas, but now she could openly ask specific questions. Simon would answer or offer his own suggestions and she could wrap up her assignment, so to speak, long before she left town.

It couldn't get much easier.

The next morning, Lisa's euphoria over the situation crashlanded the moment she saw Simon. He returned her lively greeting with a terse grunt, a frown and a furrowed brow, and a clipped, 'I'll be in my office.'

'What's with him?' SueEllen asked.

Lisa shrugged, still amazed at how he'd changed overnight. After she'd spilled her sordid history at the mall, she'd expected him to be more forthcoming with his personal details. Maybe he needed a little urging.

She entered his office. 'Is something wrong? Something you'd like to talk about?'

'No.' He fired the word like a bullet.

She recoiled under his sharp tone. Retreat was definitely in order. 'I'm a good listener,' she said softly. 'If you need help with something—'

'Everything's under control.'

Obviously things weren't if his bark was any indication, but she wouldn't go where angels feared to tread. 'OK.'

As she returned to the office area to call their first patient, her anger started to build. To think she'd trusted him enough to hear her sad life story and he didn't trust her enough to reciprocate. If he wanted privacy, she'd give him all the privacy he could possibly want.

For the rest of the morning, she kept out of his path and spoke only when necessary. He could suffer through whatever had tied his knickers in a knot on his own.

When Lorna Rajewski's mammography report came over the fax machine near the end of the day, SueEllen approached Lisa. 'Would you beard the lion in his den and give him this?'

'Are you kidding? My suit of armour is almost dented beyond repair. I don't think it can stand another blow.'

'Tell me about it. At least he's not complaining about your work. I've been on the carpet three times this afternoon for everything from losing reports to cutting off his last incoming call. It was an accident and I apologized, but you'd think I'd single-handedly spread the Black Death.'

'I may not be getting chewed, but he looks at me like he could start any time.'

SueEllen thrust out the page. 'Please? I'll owe you one.'

Lisa reluctantly took the form. 'This is against my better judgement.'

'You're a good person, Lisa Mallory. Now, I'm going to get out of here and start my weekend while I still have a few ounces of self-esteem left. If we're lucky, whatever is bothering him will be out of his system by Monday.'

'We can hope.'

Lisa trudged toward his office. The fact that the door remained closed when it normally stood wide open gave her a sense of foreboding. She knocked twice.

'Come in.'

She hurried across the room to Simon's desk and handed over the report. 'That's it for today,' she said, backing away for a quick and easy escape. 'See you Monday.'

He stood. 'Wait.'

Lisa halted in her tracks, wondering what would happen next. As far as she knew, she'd handled everything by the proverbial book. If he'd found fault, he would have had to search far and wide.

'Is your offer to help me with a problem still good?'

She had a hard time reconciling his question to his actions of the day and wondered where her generosity would lead her. 'Yes.'

His brown eyes seemed to grow darker as he fixed his unwavering gaze on hers. 'Will you come away with me for the weekend?'

CHAPTER FOUR

'COME away with you?' Surely she'd heard wrong. 'Are you serious?'

Simon sounded matter-of-fact. 'You said you'd help me if I had a problem. I know this sounds crazy, but I'm desperate. I don't know of another woman to ask. I need someone who's…discreet.'

'You want a woman to spend the weekend with you and not tell a soul about it.'

'I don't mind if anyone knows,' he corrected. 'As long as the reason behind it isn't divulged.'

'I'm flattered you chose me.' Lisa let her sarcasm show. She'd always thought such requests were made for other reasons than an ability to be circumspect.

'I realize it's short notice, but all I need is a few days of your time.'

The idea of being a short-term solution to suspicious circumstances didn't sit well.

'If we leave this evening,' he continued, apparently oblivious to her stiffened spine, 'we can be back by Sunday afternoon at the latest. I'll take care of all the arrangements. After that, I won't bother you again.'

'So I'm just supposed to drop everything to spend *one* weekend with you?'

He had the grace to appear startled and a tinge of red spread upwards from his neck. 'I'm sorry I misread the sincerity in your offer,' he said stiffly.

Not liking his implication, she bristled like a porcupine. 'I was very sincere. Even though I got dumped for another woman, I am not ripe for having a *discreet* liaison with someone I hardly know. I do have principles.'

Incensed, she stormed out of his office to seek refuge in the women's lounge. To think she'd painted Simon Travers as a model of gentlemanly behavior. With her track record in male relationships, she'd be better off entering a convent.

Admittedly, she'd imagined him in Lorna Rajewski's honeymoon suite, but her fantasy had also included a courtship of some sort. She'd pictured them spending time together, going on picnics and to movies, meeting each other's families and progressing to the point where they could read each other's thoughts.

Never had she dreamed that an opportunity for knowledge in the biblical sense would come before all else.

Before she could barricade herself behind locked doors and regain her composure, a hand latched onto her arm. She knew the owner even before she was twirled to face him.

'What's this about a weekend affair?' he asked, his brow furrowed in obvious puzzlement.

'You tell me,' she retorted. 'You ask me to go away with you because of your "problem", which no one is to know about. What assumptions would you make if the situation were reversed?'

He let go of her arm and had the grace to appear chagrined. 'It seems I didn't explain well enough.'

'Oh, really.'

'I apologize for giving you the wrong impression. My mind has been running in a hundred different directions today and I jumped ahead of myself.'

His hangdog expression softened her ire to a degree. If his private disaster had scattered his brains, she couldn't stay angry. She'd travelled in those moccasins for several miles herself.

'Apology accepted.'

He glanced at his watch. 'I don't have time to go into detail right now—'

'You'd better *make* time if you want me to go along on your joy ride.'

He ran his fingers through his hair and visibly drew a breath. His eyes appeared haunted and Lisa had the feeling he was about to unburden himself.

Unfortunately, SueEllen appeared in the hallway and Simon's apparent weak moment passed. 'With or without you,' he said firmly, 'I have to leave town in an hour. Can you trust me enough to let me explain everything on the way?'

She must be losing her grip on reality because she felt her resolve weakening. 'No secrets whatsoever?'

'No secrets,' he echoed.

The prospect of knowing all there was to know about this man enticed her like a giant box of chocolate-covered caramels.

'I promise there won't be any nefarious or immoral activities taking place,' he added.

Now she was embarrassed. What must he think of her for jumping to such a conclusion? Now he would know, or at least guess, that she found him attractive enough for her thoughts to wander along such a path.

On the other hand, what better way to work on her Christmas assignment than to be in his proverbial hip pocket for a weekend?

No one would miss her if she skipped town for the next few days. The most pressing item on her agenda had been to buy her mother's gift, and she'd already taken care of that detail. Laundry and housework were the only chores claiming her attention and she didn't mind postponing those tasks in favor of something more…interesting.

Everyone had been telling her in recent months to live a little. Now was apparently her golden opportunity.

What better way to prove that Bryan's life didn't interest her than to leave town with a gorgeous hunk, and a doctor to boot! No one needed to know their purpose...whatever it was... The less said, the better. People could draw their own conclusions.

'Can you at least tell me *where* we're going? It would be nice to know what to pack.'

Her question—and the implied decision to accompany him—erased the tension lines on his face. 'It's a little town in the Ozarks called Piney Hollow. It's fairly isolated, which translates into a definite lack in the social amenities.'

Although she'd never visited the place, she'd heard its name mentioned and knew its vicinity. 'Casual clothes, I presume?' she asked, thinking of the three-hour drive.

He nodded.

'Do you want me to meet you back here or—?'

'I'll pick you up at your house,' he told her.

'My address is—'

'3521 Aspen Road.' At her look of surprise, a small, somewhat sheepish smile tugged at his mouth. 'I was pretty sure you'd say yes, so I'd already looked it up in the phone book.'

'You were pretty sure?' she sputtered. She really must have fallen into a deep rut if a man who knew so little about her could read her so well.

He shrugged. 'More like wishful thinking.'

'Oh.' She didn't know what to say.

Simon glanced at his watch again. 'I'll see you at six.'

As she hurried to her car and zoomed toward home, Simon's potential problems filled her thoughts. It was obviously serious, whatever it was, and carried all the earmarks of an *adventure*.

Once news of this leaked out—news of the trip itself, that was—no one could say she remained stuck in the past.

It empowered her to know how she would show the gossip-mongers they were wrong about her. She was in control of her destiny and it felt wonderful.

Simon's life had rapidly spun out of control. Just when he'd thought the proverbial storm had passed, the hurricane had returned with a vengeance.

But there was no point in dwelling on what might have been. It had always been his job to deal with whatever crisis affected his immediate family, and this was just another in a long line.

He'd taken a calculated risk by asking Lisa to accompany him. The last woman who'd expected him to turn his back on his only sister whenever she needed him had left tire tracks in her haste to leave. Lisa possessed a more nurturing temperament, and he'd been fairly certain of her willingness to help. Although he'd also learned not to make any assumptions, her initial reluctance had come as a surprise. Of course, she'd acted on an erroneous assumption, but it had been his fault for not explaining adequately in the first place.

And thinking of assumptions… He grinned. Spending a weekend with Lisa would be like a dream come true, but he knew better than to ask. Any thoughts of Lisa included hearth and home and he couldn't give her those things in the near future. It wouldn't be fair to raise her hopes, then dash them.

Simon pulled into one of the two parking stalls designated for apartment 3521, glad she'd agreed to come along. He could have managed this trip alone, and if it hadn't been for his niece and nephew he would have. Lisa was great with kids and he was counting on her to lessen the trauma of being uprooted on such short notice.

She came out of the building before he could switch off the engine, clutching an overnight bag in one hand and a small ice chest in the other.

Simon met her at the curb. 'You must have been waiting.'

'Actually, I'd just finished throwing together a snack for us when I saw you drive up. If you'll take this, I'll run back upstairs and lock my door.' Without waiting for him to disagree, she thrust her things at him, then hurried inside.

For a few seconds he watched her walk away. Night fell early at this time of year, but even under the harsh glow of the entrance light and the shadows it threw he was dazzled by the vision of long legs encased in form-fitting jeans. Her uniforms certainly didn't do her justice, which was just as well. His patients required his attention—his nurse didn't.

A twinge of regret pierced his midsection...

By the time he'd stowed her gear in the trunk, placed both his parka and the ice chest in the back seat, she'd returned.

'All set,' she said, sounding breathless as she fastened her seat belt.

'I appreciate you being so prompt.' Simon reversed to re-enter the lane of traffic and navigated the maze of streets winding through the apartment complex.

'You said you were in a hurry,' she reminded him.

'I did, didn't I?' He drove through town to reach the Interstate 44 southbound exit, deferring his story until their trip was well under way.

'I didn't think you'd want to stop for dinner, so I took the liberty of throwing together a few sandwiches for us,' she said. 'I hope you don't mind. Lunchtime is hit and miss, so I'm usually starving by evening.'

'I have the same problem so, yeah, I'm glad you thought about food. It completely slipped my mind, although I did bring a few cans of grape soda.'

'Grape?' she asked. 'I thought you'd be a Dr Pepper fan.'

'I am, but I'd run out,' Simon confessed. Actually, if anyone looked in his pantry, they'd find a lot of things missing. He'd remedy that on Sunday.

'I'm not picky myself. Just so you'll know, I brought bottled water.'

Simon devoted his attention to the roadway until he'd successfully entered the closest driving lane. Several miles later the traffic had thinned out, and he activated his cruise control.

'I realize this seems rather secretive and clandestine,' he began, 'but there's a reason behind it.'

Lisa shifted positions until her knee rested dangerously close to his thigh. 'I'll hold anything you tell me in the strictest confidence.'

'Thank you.' He flexed his shoulders before he began, glad for nightfall. Somehow it was easier to divulge his secrets while cloaked in darkness. 'Have you heard of Patsy Carter?'

Lisa sat up as straight as the shoulder harness would allow. 'The country-and-western singer?'

'Yes. She's my sister.'

'Oh, my gosh. This is incredible. Wow. I have two of her CDs. Why haven't you told anyone?'

'Because we both value our privacy,' he said. 'With everything that's happened lately, neither of us wanted or needed the extra stress of unwanted publicity.'

Lisa fell silent, trying to recover from the news he'd just imparted. The complete dearth of anything personal in his office now made sense. Of course he couldn't have photos of his sister and her family on his desk. As they were famous, they would have been easily recognized.

'Wasn't her husband killed?'

'His twin-engine plane crashed on his way home from one of her concerts. It's their first Christmas without him.'

Lisa felt a new sympathy for the woman whose music she enjoyed. No wonder Simon understood her own feelings about Christmas. It didn't require any stretch of the imagination to know how Patsy must feel at this time of year.

'She's had a tough time since it happened,' he added. 'She was coming out of her grief and had even started singing again. Not professionally, but working in her home studio. I was very encouraged.'

'But now there's a crisis.'

Simon nodded. 'I got a call from her neighbour before I came to work this morning. Apparently she hadn't picked up her mail for the last few days and they wondered if she'd gone out of town and had forgotten to tell them.

'Then her publicist telephoned. He'd been trying to reach her and couldn't. I immediately called her neighbours back—they keep an eye on things when Patsy's on tour—and asked them to check on her.'

He fell silent and Lisa waited for him to continue.

'By the time I got in touch with the Willsons, it was late afternoon. They found her, but she was totally inebriated and barely functioning. The kids have apparently been fending for themselves, which, for a three- and a five-year-old, doesn't say much.'

Lisa winced at the thought.

'It was bad enough,' he continued, 'that Mrs Willson threatened to notify the Child Welfare Services if I didn't immediately take charge of the situation. I'd already planned to drive up this evening, but when I heard that I knew things were much more serious than I'd imagined.'

Lisa shuddered, thinking of how the tabloids and news media would have a heyday if even a whisper of Patsy's fall from grace leaked out.

He shook his head. 'I should have seen this coming. Anticipated it somehow.'

'Why?' she asked bluntly. 'You're not a psychiatrist, psychologist or even a therapist.'

'No, but I talk to her three times a week. I should have suspected something was going on inside her head, that she wasn't over her grief.'

'Don't be so hard on yourself. The stress of the holidays probably overwhelmed her to the point where she couldn't cope. The main thing is that you're arranging for her to have professional help.' She narrowed her eyes. 'You are, aren't you?'

He sounded tired. 'I'm checking Patsy into a private clinic tomorrow morning. Afterwards, I'm bringing the kids home with me. Courtney and Kyle have stayed at my house before, so it won't be like they're moving to a strange place.'

He glanced in her direction. 'Whenever they've visited me, we've turned it into an adventure because I don't own a lot of furniture. However, I can't expect them to sleep on the floor for six weeks. Or longer.'

'A bed would be nice,' Lisa agreed.

'As I said, they'll need all sorts of things that I might not think important, but which a woman would. I know I'm asking a lot, but I need your help and insight to make this transition easier for them.'

After hearing this story, she couldn't refuse—she didn't even consider it. 'I'm glad you asked me,' she said, knowing how hard his choice must have weighed on him. Not only had he had to admit his inability to handle the situation on his own, but he'd also had to surrender his well-guarded secrets.

'I doubt if we'll transform my house from austere bachelor quarters to one completely fit for children on Sunday,' he mused, 'but if you'll get me started and make out a list I can do the rest.'

She wanted to jump in and offer to help for as long as he needed her, but his tone stopped her. Apparently, come Sunday evening, he planned to have his life under control once again. Simon possessed the traits of independence and self-sufficiency to a fault and wouldn't appreciate her meddling in his affairs, even if he *had* included her so far.

'Let's deal with Sunday on Sunday,' Lisa said pragmatically. Although she wanted to do whatever she could, a lot depended upon the children's reaction. Having a strange person underfoot, even if their uncle was nearby, might not be for the best.

She'd simply be patient and play this particular tune by ear.

The headlights from the car following them illuminated the interior just enough for her to see that the harsh lines around Simon's eyes had softened.

'Not to be nosy, but where are your parents? The in-laws?'

'Our dad died when I was little. Mom passed away when I was eighteen and so I assumed responsibility for Patsy. Her parents-in-law are both in poor health and live in an assisted living complex in St Louis. Neither are in any physical shape to handle two small children, even well-behaved ones.'

She thought of her own network of family. 'No aunts? Uncles? Cousins?'

'I take care of my own.'

His calm statement sent an odd shiver down her spine. She wondered what it would be like to be so cherished that he would always be there, no matter what. Jealousy over his future wife—whoever the lucky lady would be—reared its head.

Those few words also said more than a lengthy explanation could have revealed. Apparently the remaining relatives weren't ones Simon thought worth mentioning. His next comment confirmed it.

'We managed without them for years. Why should I involve them now?'

Unbidden, a picture of Simon as a young man came to Lisa's mind. It must have been difficult to support himself and his younger sister and still go to school while his close kin apparently turned their backs on them. And now, twelve years later, Simon continued to fill those shoes for his sister whenever necessary.

But who supported Simon when he had a problem?

He had to have them. Everyone did, at one point or another—no one was immune. To her knowledge, he didn't have a soul with whom he could share his disappointments or his successes.

Her heart swelled with pride to think that, of all the people in Farmington, he'd included *her* in his tight family circle.

She reached out and touched his arm as his hand rested on the steering-wheel. 'Don't worry. I'll be around as long as you want me to be.'

If they parted ways on Sunday, she could live with it, but at least Simon now understood the open-endedness of her offer.

He nodded to acknowledge her comment. 'I just hope I can provide what Courtney and Kyle need in their life right now.'

His insecurity caught her by surprise and touched her heart. As a man who dealt calmly with people's lives, sometimes making the difference between life and death, he'd never struck her as being insecure about anything. Hearing Simon voice his own doubts made him seem more human and...vulnerable.

Get a grip, she scolded herself. It wouldn't do for her to fall in love with her boss, no matter how attracted she was to him. The problems would be insurmountable, not to mention devastating. She would help him with his niece and nephew then go on her cruise. When she returned life would return to the way it had been.

'You're physically providing for them,' she said slowly, 'which is important. Right now, I'd say they need a whole lot of love and understanding, and I suspect that Uncle Simon has plenty to give.'

He didn't answer.

Sensing it was time to lighten the mood, she reached into the back seat and retrieved her ice chest. There was nothing like focusing on the mundane to pull one out of the doldrums. 'I'm starving. Shall we eat?'

At nine o'clock, Simon pulled into the meandering drive leading to his sister's home. The twin beams of his headlights pierced the darkness of the tree-lined gravel road as it twisted and turned through various gullies and hills.

'I'm anxious to see this in the daytime,' Lisa commented.

'It's beautiful during the summer,' he remarked as he followed the trail down another gully.

Lisa peered through the trees, searching for signs of other human life. 'I don't see any lights out here,' she said.

'Because there aren't any. The Willsons live in the house at the intersection of this road and the main highway. Patsy's husband bought the land north of the Willsons' property and built the house in the middle of his section in order to have privacy.'

'He certainly succeeded.' No one would ever have known that anyone lived back here, much less a famous singer.

'We're almost there,' he said.

Lisa strained her eyes to catch her first glimpse of what was probably a mansion. She wasn't disappointed.

A huge home, built to resemble a log cabin and blend into the scenery, rose in front of her. A three-foot-tall chain-link fence surrounded the well-lit property, probably in an attempt to keep the children confined and wild animals out rather than to deter snoopy and unwanted people.

The tires crunched on the gravel as Simon parked on the circular driveway in front of the house.

'It's picture-perfect.'

Thanks to the yard lights, she saw the tension lines on Simon's face reappear. His whole body seemed stiff.

Lisa couldn't stop herself. She reached out and grabbed his hand. 'No matter what we find inside, it will be OK.'

'Yeah, I know.'

'It may be hard, but you're not alone,' she added. 'A burden shared is only half a burden.'

He managed a smile before he opened his door and unfolded himself from the car.

By the time they reached the massive front door, with its carved adornments and stained glass window, it was as if Simon's vulnerability had completely disappeared. In the space of those few feet and several seconds, he had squared his shoulders and in so doing reminded her of a sturdy warrior prepared to handle anything.

He put his hand out to knock, but before he could make contact the door flew open to reveal a short, grandmotherly-type woman.

'Thank goodness you're here,' she said, stepping aside to allow them entrance.

Simon ushered Lisa inside before him and helped her remove her coat. 'How's Patsy?'

Standing in the foyer, Lisa listened to their conversation with half an ear while she took in her surroundings. A long flight of stairs curved upward on her right, its solid oak bannister an example of skilled craftsmanship and beauty. To the left was the formal living room where a black baby grand piano seemed to beg for attention. She couldn't wait to explore the rest of the house tomorrow.

'She's in the kitchen. A-floatin' in coffee, but we haven't dared to leave her alone.'

Simon disappeared into the living room and through another doorway, presumably headed in the right direction.

Since he hadn't introduced her, Lisa took care it herself. 'I'm Lisa Mallory,' she said, extending her hand. 'I work with Dr Travers as his nurse. You must be Mrs Willson.'

'Just call me Eula May,' the older woman replied, her grip solid. 'I'm powerful glad you came along with him. Simon's got plenty on his plate right now and it'll be easier if'n he can spread the bitter helpin's around a bit.'

'This won't be easy for any of them,' Lisa agreed.

'I hope he's not mad at me for threatenin' to call the Child Services, but the condition those poor tykes was in just about broke my heart. I was afraid he'd think my Hank and I was just over-reactin' about Patsy.'

'He's not angry with you,' Lisa told her. 'I think he's angry with himself for not seeing that this was coming.'

'Well, he shouldn't,' Eula May declared. 'Patsy's had a tough time since Mick passed on, but here lately she'd acted like she'd accepted her loss. I guess not.'

'Simon will see she gets the help she needs,' Lisa said. 'Where are Courtney and Kyle?'

'Sleeping. They stuffed themselves at supper, then dozed off, so I tucked them in their beds. Poor babes couldn't have ate more'n cereal and snack food for the past three days. Should have checked on 'em sooner, I suppose, but I hate to butt in all the time.'

Simon returned with Eula May's husband, Hank. He was a little taller than the short Eula May, wore a pair of overalls and a red plaid flannel shirt, and was nearly bald. His eyes reflected both kindness and worry.

'I appreciate all your help,' Simon told the couple. 'We'll close the house and take the children home with us. If you can keep an eye on the property and forward Patsy's mail to me, I'd appreciate it.'

Hank nodded. 'Come, Mother. Let's go on home.' He opened the closet in the foyer and removed two well-worn parkas. The snags and small rips in the fabric indicated they'd seen a lot of duty.

Eula May slipped her arms in her coat and snapped it closed. 'Now, if ya need us, we're just up the road.'

'We'll be fine. Lisa and I will take over from here.'

'G'night to ya both,' Hank said as he urged his wife to the door.

After everyone had echoed their goodbyes, the house fell ominously silent as Simon and Lisa exchanged glances. The tick of the grandfather clock sounded louder than normal until the Westminster chime on the half-hour broke in.

'Is she OK?' Lisa asked tentatively.

'She's sober, but I'm going to stay up with her for a while. There's a spare room next to Kyle's. Help yourself to whatever you need.'

'And you?'

He sighed. 'Patsy refuses to go to bed, so I'll try to get her to rest on the sofa.' His grin seemed rather half-hearted. 'The recliners aren't too bad.'

'I'll bring in our bags.'

'I can get them. If you don't mind staying with Patsy?'

'She doesn't need a stranger right now,' Lisa said, trying to put herself in Patsy's shoes. 'She needs you. I can manage two overnight bags, and if I can't then it's time I started lifting weights.'

'OK. If you need coffee, I just made a fresh pot.'

'Thanks, but I think I'll pass on the caffeine for now.'

Lisa slipped on her coat and returned outside. The temperature had dropped further and her breath left little white trails in the night air. She balanced the bags, her purse and the ice chest, then hurried back inside. After hanging her coat in the closet, she left Simon's bag and the ice chest near the door, and went upstairs in search of her temporary quarters.

Feeling both mentally and physically drained, Lisa vowed to sleep a few hours before taking her turn at Patsy-watch duty. Simon needed his rest, too, and although he might argue she decided she wouldn't take no for an answer.

She ascended the steps to the second level. Turning on the overhead hall light, she opened the first door on the right. It was huge and boasted a king-sized bed. Obviously the master bedroom.

The next room was blue and boyish and a small form lay huddled underneath a bedspread decorated with soccer balls. Lisa gently closed the door and moved to the room across the way.

A canopy bed with pink coverings stood in her line of vision. Courtney's bare legs showed underneath her yellow nightie and the comforter lay on a heap to one side of the full-sized bed. Lisa tiptoed in to cover the child, but as she did Courtney restlessly moved her legs. Whimpers came from her throat and she flung out her arms.

Thinking the child was caught in the throes of a nightmare, Lisa crooned softly as she touched her forehead.

Her skin was hot and dry.

Lisa's nursing instincts took over and she gently ran her hands over Courtney's face, before noting her quick, shallow respirations and rapid pulse.

Immediately she covered the little girl with a sheet and went in search of Simon. She found him in the kitchen with a wan-faced woman who bore a striking similarity to him. Before Lisa could say anything, Simon asked, 'Can you help Patsy pack a bag?'

Lisa stared at him. 'Right now?' It was ten o'clock.

'She's agreed to enter treatment, so I'm taking her to a private clinic near Branson. I called and they're expecting us.'

Lisa glanced at the thin woman who hardly resembled the vibrant personality featured on her CD covers. 'Yeah, sure, but can I talk to you first?' she asked. 'In private?'

She must have telegraphed enough urgency in her voice because he agreed without argument. He followed her into the living room.

'You can't take her tonight,' Lisa whispered.

'Why not?'

'Because Courtney's sick.'

CHAPTER FIVE

SIMON's eyes widened. 'Sick?'

Lisa kept her voice low, conscious of Patsy only a few feet away. 'I don't have a thermometer, but I'd say Courtney has at least a 102 degree temp. Her respirations are fast and shallow. Her pulse is rapid.'

'Are you sure?'

She shot him a look. 'I'm a nurse. I can tell a fever when I feel one.'

'Damn.' He rubbed the back of his neck.

'You can't send Patsy away without telling her first. She *is* Courtney's mother.'

'If she knows, she won't go,' he said flatly. 'And Patsy definitely needs treatment.'

'I agree, but if she ever learns how you kept this from her, she'll never forgive you, Simon.'

He rubbed the back of his neck, his frustration evident in his face.

'Not only that, but it isn't fair to the children to spirit their mother out of the house while they're asleep. Do you want them to be afraid to close their eyes because when they do someone they love disappears?'

'No,' he said slowly.

'Then let them say their goodbyes and hear her assurances that she's coming back.'

'Checking into the clinic at this time of night will protect Patsy's privacy the most,' he argued.

'Probably. But Patsy isn't the only one you have to consider. You asked me to make this situation less traumatic for the children,' she reminded him, 'and I'm telling you they'll suffer more if they wake up in the morning and she's gone without a farewell. How will you compensate for their feelings of desertion?'

He didn't answer and she pressed on.

'As long as she's alert, it's not your decision to make,' she said softly. 'Patsy probably feels as if she's lost control of her life. Don't take this from her, too.'

He didn't agree or disagree. Instead, he said, 'I'll check on Courtney.'

'OK.'

Simon went upstairs and Lisa returned to the kitchen. For lack of anything else to do—she didn't want anything to drink, especially not coffee—she took the chair Simon had vacated. 'Hi. I'm Lisa.'

Patsy sniffled. Her long dark hair hung limply around her tear-streaked face. 'I know. Simon's told me about you. You work for him, right?'

'I'm his office nurse.'

Patsy glanced around. 'Where did he go?'

'To check on the kids. He'll be right back.'

She raised her bloodshot eyes to meet Lisa's gaze. 'They're OK, aren't they?'

'Everything's under control.' Lisa changed the subject. 'You have a lovely home.'

'Mick and I spent a lot of hours planning it,' Patsy said as she outlined the rim of her mug with a trembling finger. 'It was our dream house.'

'It's beautiful. Did you do the work yourself?'

Patsy shook her head. 'My schedule didn't allow it. We hired a construction company and an interior decorator, but we chose everything right down to the doorknobs.'

Simon reappeared in the kitchen, carrying Courtney. The little girl's face was flushed, her long curly blonde locks tousled, and she clung to him as if she was afraid to let go. His face was troubled, and as he sat on Patsy's left Lisa knew he'd decided to break the news to her.

'I don't want you to worry, but Courtney's running a temperature,' he began. 'Has she been complaining of anything in particular the last few days?'

Patsy's chin trembled as she stared at her daughter resting her head against Simon's chest. She reached across the table to stroke Courtney's baby-fine hair. 'Not to my knowledge, but, then, she might have and I didn't notice. What's wrong with her?'

'It might be strep throat.'

She swiped her eyes. 'This is all my fault.'

'Kids get strep all the time,' Simon said, his voice low and calm. 'Court's going to be fine. I'll start her on antibiotics right away and she'll be running around as usual within forty-eight hours.'

'I can't leave them now.'

'Maybe not at the moment,' he conceded with a sharp glance at Lisa, 'but you'll have to go tomorrow.'

Tears glistened in Patsy's eyes. 'Why can't I wait until next week?'

'Because I can't stay that long,' he said, patting Courtney's back. 'And you're not capable of being here by yourself. Mrs Willson can't do it either. We've already discussed your other alternative.'

Lisa guessed it pertained to the Child Welfare Department. The choice between voluntarily relinquishing her children to Simon's care versus the nightmare of involving the court system wasn't a difficult one to make.

Patsy rose on unsteady feet. 'I'll put her to bed.'

Lisa exchanged a glance with Simon. He clearly wasn't happy with the turn of events. 'Let Lisa carry her,' he said.

Patsy nodded as if she understood that she was too unsteady for the task, and he handed Courtney into Lisa's arms. Lisa settled her against her chest, touched by the trusting way the child snuggled against her.

'Is there a pharmacy near by?' he asked.

Patsy shook her head. 'A nurse practitioner staffs our local health clinic. She might have the medicine you want. Her number's in the phone book.'

Simon riffled through the drawer underneath the wall phone while Lisa joined Patsy to go upstairs. Patsy's unsteady gait warned Lisa to stay close. It would be terrible if the woman fell down the stairs.

Once inside Courtney's room, Lisa placed the little girl on the bed before Patsy sat next to her and stroked her forehead. Even under the nightlight's faint glow, the love she had for her daughter showed on her face. Love and regret.

Courtney stirred. 'Mommy. My froat hurts.'

'I know, sweetie.'

'Am I sick?'

'Just a little. Uncle Simon is here and he's going to make you all better.'

'He tolded me.' She paused. 'I'm hot. Firsty, too.'

Patsy glanced at Lisa, and after a wordless exchange Lisa went downstairs to fetch a drink. The refrigerator was relatively bare and she searched the pantry. To her relief, she found a bottle of apple juice. After filling a cup and adding ice to chill it, she hurried back upstairs to hunt for a painreliever in the bathroom medicine cabinet. Luckily, she found a blister pack of children's-strength acetaminophen.

While Courtney sipped her drink and chewed her tablets, Kyle stumbled into the room. 'Mama?'

'Yes, honey?'

'Is it time to get up?'

'No, hon. Go back to bed.'

He yawned. 'OK.' He started to turn, then stopped. 'Mama? Are you better now?'

Patsy's smile was weak. 'A little. Why don't you come here? I have something to tell you.'

Kyle went over to her. Sensing an important moment between mother and children, Lisa remained in the background to listen and watch as Patsy gathered the two little ones close.

'Mommy has been sick and I'm going to go to a clinic to get better.'

'Is that like a hospital?' Kyle asked.

'Yes. I'll be gone for a while, but Uncle Simon and his friend, Lisa, will be taking care of you.'

'Are they staying here?'

'Uncle Simon is taking you to his house.'

'When will you come home?' Once again, Kyle was asking all of the questions.

'Soon.'

'Will you call us like when you took trips before?'

'Every chance I get,' Patsy promised.

'And then you'll be all better?'

'Yes.'

'OK.' Kyle flung his arms around his mother. 'Love you.'

'I love you, too.' Patsy's voice possessed a husky quality that hadn't been there before.

Lisa's eyes brimmed with tears over the sight she'd witnessed. Patsy was saying her goodbyes, knowing she didn't have any alternative.

'Off to bed now,' Patsy told Kyle. 'Be good for your Uncle Simon and Lisa.'

'OK.' Kyle scooted off the bed and stopped near Lisa. 'Could you tuck me in?'

Lisa was touched by his acceptance of her future role. 'I

would be honored,' she said, letting his small hand slip into hers.

A few minutes later she pulled his comforter up to his chin. 'Goodnight, Kyle. Sleep tight.'

He rolled over and promptly fell asleep.

Lisa peeked into Courtney's room and saw Patsy sitting against the headboard, cradling Courtney in her arms. 'I'm going to hold her until Simon gets here,' Patsy said.

Lisa nodded. She could understand Patsy's need to give her daughter the one thing she craved—a mother's comfort. 'Yell if you need anything.'

She went into the spare bedroom, left the door slightly ajar to hear Patsy's call or Simon's return and sat on the edge of the bed. Maybe she should indulge in a cup of black coffee because the night promised to be a long one.

A few minutes later she heard the quiet click of the door closing downstairs. She jumped to her feet and met Simon coming up the stairs with a small brown paper bag in hand.

'Any luck?'

'I brought a penicillin injection,' he said. 'It will work faster. Where's Patsy?'

'She's with Courtney.' A few minutes later, she stood next to the bed, ready to help Simon. Children were notorious for not holding still whenever needles were involved, and she was prepared to do her part.

'Should I wake her first?' Patsy asked.

'Let her sleep,' Simon advised as he ripped open wrappers. 'By the time she realizes what's happened, it will be over.'

He raised Courtney's nightie to bare her thigh. Without a word, Lisa manoeuvred herself into position and held the child's leg in a firm grip. Simon swiped a spot on her skin with an alcohol pad, then swiftly injected the contents of his syringe into the muscle.

Courtney stiffened, then let out an ear-splitting shriek. Luckily, by then the worst was over and Patsy crooned softly to soothe her. It didn't take long for Courtney's cries to diminish to small sobs.

Lisa gathered up the debris and left the room. After discarding the used supplies in the kitchen, she poured the last cup of coffee and wondered if she should make another pot. After all it was midnight and everyone needed to grab at least a few hours of sleep.

Simon walked in, looking totally drained. 'I'd offer this to you,' she said, 'but I think you'll have a caffeine high for an entire week as it is.'

'Probably so. What did you say to Patsy?'

She was startled by his question. 'Nothing. Why?'

'She's agreed to leave for Branson as soon as Courtney's fever breaks.'

Lisa eyed him cautiously. 'That's good, isn't it?'

He pinched the bridge of his nose. 'Yeah. I just expected a bigger fight over it.'

'When you were gone,' she began slowly, 'Kyle woke up and came into Courtney's room. Patsy explained about being sick, how she was going to a clinic to get better and how, until then, you'd take care of them at your house. He seemed to accept it without much question.'

Simon fell silent for a long moment before he heaved a sigh. 'I guess that's that. You'd better get some sleep. Tomorrow's going to be a busy day.'

She studied the circles under his eyes, the shadow of whiskers on his face. 'You need sleep worse than I do. Why don't you grab forty winks while I keep a watch on Courtney.'

'You go first.'

'I've caught my second wind,' she said. 'You haven't. No arguments. Nurse's orders.'

'You talked me into it, but only for a couple of hours.' He glanced at his watch. 'Wake me at three. We'll both get four hours of shut-eye.'

She rose. 'In that case, I suggest you don't waste a single minute.'

He helped her check the door locks and shut off the lights before he grabbed his bag and followed her up the stairs. At the top he hesitated as if unsure of where he should spend his next few hours.

Lisa immediately steered him toward the spare room where she'd stashed her overnight case. 'You might as well use this room since I won't. Sleep tight.'

'Don't forget. Three a.m.'

'On the dot,' she promised.

By three o'clock she was halfway through the stack of magazines she'd amassed and had decided to let Simon nap a little longer. To her surprise, he shuffled out of the room in stockinged feet, yawning as he buttoned the two middle buttons of his shirt and blinked the sleep out of his eyes.

Although he was decent, his shirt tails hung loosely over his jeans. The fabric wasn't wrinkled, which suggested that he'd taken it off before collapsing into bed.

'You're awake.' She lowered a gardening magazine and stared up at him from her spot on the hallway floor between the two children's rooms. The temperature in the house had dropped, and she'd wrapped herself in an afghan to keep warm.

'Yeah.'

'Did you set an alarm or something?'

'It's internal. A carry-over from my internship days.' His gaze narrowed. 'You weren't going to call me, were you?'

She grinned. 'I'm wide awake. It didn't make sense to drag you out of a toasty bed so I could lie there and count sheep. Courtney's fine. She's still feverish so I just gave her another dose of acetaminophen. Otherwise, she's resting quietly. So is Patsy.'

Simon held out his hand and pulled her to her feet. 'And now it's your turn,' he said. 'My gut feeling says you won't be counting as many of those sheep as you think you will.'

'We'll see.'

He pointed her toward the room he'd just vacated and nudged her forward. 'Go. I'll see you at seven.'

Suddenly the thought of resting her weary bones on a firm mattress under a warm comforter seemed like heaven. She closed the door to the cozy bedroom, slipped off her clothes, tugged a flannel, knee-length nightshirt over her head and slid under the covers, conscious of Simon's lingering scent.

She breathed deeply, certain she wouldn't catch a single wink. How could she, knowing Simon had rested his body on this exact place only moments ago? Why, even the linen held traces of his scent, and the pillows held an indentation of the shape of his head.

How ironic to accuse him of wanting a weekend affair and then wind up sharing a bed. Not at the same time, of course, but she couldn't deny the facts. They *had* shared a set of sheets.

It was something to dream about, she thought with a vague smile as she visualized four-legged woolly creatures. A pasture appeared, then gradually filled with a flock extending as far as her mind's eye could see.

She yawned and didn't count a single one.

She dreamt of white sand, sunny beaches, an endless stretch of the bluest water, and a handsome companion whose lips made her knees go weak. A flying insect of some sort interrupted her idyllic moment and she brushed it away from her mouth.

It returned to land on her nose, and she swatted at it again. Bugs didn't belong in her dreams.

'Good morning,' said the pesky fly.

Her eyelids flew open. The glow from the hallway light revealed Simon standing above her with his hair neat and his face clean-shaven.

'Morning,' she muttered, rubbing the sleep out of her eyes as she noticed the world outside her window no longer seemed as dark as it had when she'd gone to bed.

'Courtney's fever broke about six,' he said. 'Patsy is getting ready to leave. We hope to hit the road within thirty minutes or so.'

Lisa flung back the covers to rise. 'I'll fix breakfast.'

'Um, I...I've...already eaten.'

Too late, she realized her nightshirt had hiked up to mid-thigh. Although her bare legs were well within the realm of decency, she was extremely aware of Simon's gaze and how he'd never, ever seen her legs before.

She stood and the hem of her shirt came to her knees, yet somehow she sensed he could see right through the fabric. The cooler air made her shiver and she was keenly aware of his attention focusing on her chest.

'I...um...left plenty for you,' he said, seemingly reluctant to tear his gaze away from her body, although he did. 'I'll see you downstairs.'

Lisa jumped into her clothes, completed her stint in the bathroom in record time and hurried to the kitchen where she found Patsy.

The other woman looked much better than she had last night—a shower and shampoo did wonders. While her features were less haggard, she looked like an extremely tired version of the photogenic Patsy Carter.

'Where's Simon?' Lisa asked, noticing the scrambled eggs in the skillet on the stove.

'Loading the car. Before I leave, I want to tell you a few things.'

Thinking Patsy had last-minute instructions for her house and tips for the children, Lisa grabbed the phone message pad and a pen before she sat down. 'Let me jot them down so I don't forget anything important.'

Patsy placed her hand over Lisa's. 'You won't need to write this. What I have to say concerns Simon.'

Lisa laid the pen on the pad and folded her hands.

'What do you think of my brother?'

The question was a test of some sort and Lisa wasn't sure how to answer in order to pass. Telling his sister that she found him wildly attractive, that he made her hormone levels do crazy things and that being with him felt 'right' would be like playing with fire. If Patsy related her comments to Simon... Lisa didn't want to think about how ticklish things could turn.

'I only know him as my boss, but he's a wonderful man.'

'Do you like being around him? Off duty, that is?'

Warmth crept up Lisa's face as she thought of how easily her thoughts travelled in his direction. Although she'd only seen him twice outside the clinic, at the mall and now, this weekend, she intended to treasure those moments.

'This is the first time I've spent time with him, other than at work. We get along well together.' She winced at how dull she sounded, but without any encouragement from Simon she couldn't admit that she'd like something to develop between them.

Patsy's mouth formed a tight circle, as if weighing Lisa's answers. 'Simon has sacrificed himself for me time after time,' she said. 'I thought I finally had it together and now I've put him in this position again.'

Lisa didn't interrupt, but nodded for her to continue.

'Did he tell you how he worked nearly day and night

during med school to support us so I could establish my career?'

Lisa shook her head.

'I'd been singing in a local band and people encouraged me to think big. So Simon sent me to Nashville and literally browbeat music studios into producing my demo tapes. Then he pounded the pavement to find an agent who believed in me as much as he did.'

Patsy's mouth softened into a smile. 'In the end, Mick turned out to be more than just an agent and I married him. Anyway, I'm trying to say this—Simon would do anything for me, often at great personal cost.'

'I'm not surprised,' Lisa said, thinking of the facts he'd already divulged.

'Unfortunately, he has this idea about handling everything strictly by himself. Although I consider my kids to be two little angels, I'm afraid he's going to have his hands full.'

'My brother and sister both have children,' Lisa said, thinking of the merry chase her nieces and nephews led her siblings and their spouses. 'I understand completely.'

'Simon hates to ask for help. This time he's going to need all he can get.' Patsy leaned across the table. Her grip was surprisingly strong. 'Please, don't let him shoulder this alone.'

Lisa was stunned by her request. How could she promise one thing to Simon's sister when, at the same time, it went against Simon's wishes? He'd only invited her into his private life for the weekend, not for the full six or eight weeks.

'I have faith in you,' Patsy added.

'You do? Why?'

'Because Simon brought you here,' she said simply. 'He hasn't brought anyone before, so that tells me how much he trusts you. And if Simon believes in you, so do I.'

Her vote of confidence brought a lump to Lisa's throat. 'I'll help as much as he'll allow,' she said. If Simon's wishes were at odds with Patsy's, Lisa's hands were tied.

'Not good enough,' Patsy insisted.

Simon strode into the room, his cheeks red from being outside. 'What's not good enough?'

'I want your promise that you and Lisa will work together to take care of the children.'

'I won't let them play in the street,' he said lightly. 'And I promise we won't eat at McDonald's and Burger King for every meal.'

Patsy gave him a benevolent smile. 'I know, but having two children for a few days is different from being solely responsible for several weeks. I don't want you to be overwhelmed.'

'I can handle it,' he began, casting a strange look in Lisa's direction. Afraid he might accuse her of manipulating events, Lisa shrugged, hoping he would realize how Patsy's request had shocked her, too.

'I'm sure you can,' Patsy said, 'but I want Courtney and Kyle to have a woman's touch while I'm gone.'

His hesitation spoke volumes. Simon obviously intended Lisa and he to part company after they'd settled the pair in his home on Sunday.

Patsy must have thought the same way. 'If not, I'll call Child Welfare Services myself, so they'll be in a foster home.'

Lisa rose, feeling a desperate desire to escape. 'Maybe I should leave so you two can discuss this privately.'

'No,' Patsy said, firmly. 'I want you here.'

Lisa slowly lowered herself onto the chair.

Simon's hazel eyes narrowed as he studied his sister. 'You're bluffing.'

'I'm serious. I know what your work and on-call schedule can be like. The children would feel more secure when you were gone if Lisa was a constant presence.'

A muscle tightened in his jaw, but it didn't take him long to voice a decision. 'OK,' he said gruffly. 'If it will give you peace of mind…'

Relief appeared on his sister's face. 'It will. Then I'm ready to go.'

She rose and faced Lisa. Her mouth quivered with a tremulous smile and a sheen of tears glistened in the pair of eyes identical to Simon's. 'Take care of my babies,' she said hoarsely.

Lisa hugged her. 'I will. We will.'

Patsy broke away and headed for the door. Simon cast a helpless glance at Lisa before he followed. As Lisa watched the two drive away in the early morning light, she wondered if she could have acted so selflessly had their roles been reversed.

'I won't let you down,' she vowed aloud to the empty room. Simon might be her biggest obstacle if he truly didn't want her help, but 'stubborn' was her middle name. She doubted if he knew about her tendency toward perseverance, but he would learn.

He would also do well to learn quickly.

CHAPTER SIX

'WHEN'S Unca Simon coming back?' Kyle's voice held a distinct whine as he carefully fished the letter K out of his bowl of alphabet soup.

Lisa ladled a smaller portion for Courtney. She carried the dish from the stove to the table, where one clearly bored young man and one sickly little girl sat staring at her.

'Soon,' she said, placing Courtney's lunch in front of her. The little girl eyed it with some doubt.

'It's smoking,' Courtney announced in her hoarse whisper.

'Not for long,' Lisa said cheerfully, using a trick she'd learned from caring for her sister's children. She gathered a few chips of ice out of the trays in the freezer and carefully dropped them into the soup. 'By the time the ice melts, your food will be the perfect temperature.'

'I don't like this,' Kyle informed her as he picked a Y out of his lunch.

'Really?' Lisa asked, sitting next to Courtney.

'Yeah. We have it all the time.'

That explained why there were six cans in the pantry. Clearly, Patsy didn't cook a lot of her meals from scratch. At least, not lately.

'What *do* you like to eat?' she countered.

'Pizza,' Kyle answered, his face brightening as he carefully removed an L shape and lined it up near the other letters on his saucer.

'S'ghetti,' Courtney chimed in.

'I'll see what I can do for dinner,' Lisa said, already

86

thinking ahead to their next meal. The cupboards were on the bare side and the refrigerator wasn't in much better shape. Apparently Patsy's decline had been rapid during the past week because the freezer compartment only held a half-eaten carton of ice cream, several trays of ice cubes and a package of strawberries.

A single apple, two oranges, three limp carrots and a soggy head of lettuce lay forlornly in their bins. The meat situation was dire, but at least she had a full dozen eggs and a brick of cheese to work with.

If the worst came to the worst, she'd call Eula May for directions to the nearest grocery store. Somehow Lisa doubted if Patsy would mind if she borrowed her car for an emergency run.

'How do you spell your name?' Kyle asked.

'L, I, S, A.'

Kyle began sorting through the pasta shapes on his spoon before he ate. With his face wrinkled in concentration and the tip of his tongue sticking out of his mouth, he studiously searched for the letters Lisa had indicated.

Before Lisa could sample her own lunch, Courtney slid off her chair to stand next to her. She raised her arms.

It didn't require motherhood to know what the child wanted. Lisa lifted her onto her lap. 'Aren't you hungry?'

Courtney shook her head and burrowed her face against Lisa's chest.

'Why don't you try a taste?' Lisa suggested, pulling the bowl forward. 'This looks absolutely delicious.'

She dipped the spoon into the beef broth and brought it to Courtney's lips. 'Beep, beep.'

A tiny smile appeared and Courtney obediently opened her mouth like a baby bird.

'Do you think Unca Simon will get here before dark?' Kyle asked.

'I'm sure he will,' Lisa said calmly, hoping he wouldn't make her eat her words. She fed Courtney another spoonful, more interested in getting fluids into the child than anything else.

'Will we go to his house right away, or stay here for a few days?'

'If it's not too late when your uncle gets back, we may leave tonight,' Lisa said, pleased by the amount of liquid Courtney had swallowed. 'Otherwise we'll leave first thing in the morning.'

'But what about our stuff?' His big brown eyes didn't waver from hers as he bit into his peanut butter and jelly sandwich.

'We'll pack after your naps.' Lisa watched Courtney yawn and her eyelids droop. Holding this precious little one was such a joy. She'd expected more resistance from the kids—she was a stranger, after all—but they'd accepted her presence without question or argument.

Kyle sat up straight. 'I'm too old for a nap. I'm *five*.'

Lisa pretended to think. 'That's right. How could I have forgotten? You don't have to sleep.'

Kyle preened.

'You just need to rest.' As a stubborn expression settled on his face, Lisa hurried to add, 'Grown-ups take time to rest even while they're at work.'

His eyes grew wide. 'They do?'

'We call them coffee-breaks. It's supposed to recharge our mental and physical batteries.' Whenever we can take them, that is, she finished silently.

'So mine can be like a grown-up coffee-break?'

'Yes.'

His expression became thoughtful. 'What do you do when you take a coffee-break? Besides drink coffee.'

Lisa grinned. 'We visit with the other people who are

taking one at the same time. I like to look at a magazine, plan my shopping list, that sort of thing.'

His eyes sparkled with excitement. 'I can write down what I want to take with me.'

Lisa doubted if Kyle's list would be one that she—or anyone other than Kyle—could read. However, she wasn't about to dampen his enthusiasm. 'An excellent idea. You can make a list of Courtney's favorite toys, too. She's not feeling well and might forget something important.'

'OK.'

Lisa slowly rose, cradling Courtney close. 'Why don't we go on upstairs and take our breaks now? When we're finished, we'll start to work.'

Kyle scooted away from the table. 'Wouldn't it be neat if we were all packed and ready to go when Unca Simon got here?'

'Wouldn't it?' she agreed, hoping for Simon to miraculously walk through the door. Although she didn't have any qualms about gathering whatever the children needed, it would be nice to know if she should include items other than the obvious clothing and toys.

If his bachelor pad resembled her brother's, Simon wouldn't own enough towels, dishes and cutlery to accommodate two extra people, even if they were pint-sized.

She'd start with the obvious and keep her fingers crossed for Simon's arrival before the question of the other necessities arose.

Lisa tucked Courtney into bed and covered her with a lightweight blanket. Next, she went into Kyle's room and found him lying on his stomach on top of his comforter, his pencil scratching furiously across a yellow tablet.

'I'm making my list,' he said seriously. 'See?' He held up the pad to show off his squiggles and pictures.

'You're doing a wonderful job. I'll call you as soon as the coffee-break is over.'

'OK.'

She closed the door behind him, guessing he'd doze off and give her about ninety minutes without interruption. This morning, before the children had risen, she'd tidied Patsy's room and washed the bedding. Someone would probably arrange for the house to be aired before the family returned, but at least Lisa could leave it in relative order. She hated to leave a mess in her own home, and she wouldn't do it in someone else's.

Lisa crept downstairs and restored the kitchen to rights while she nibbled on a piece of cheese. Although it was two o'clock, she wasn't particularly worried over Simon's absence. The paperwork for Patsy's admission and a discussion of her treatment plan could take hours to complete.

By three-thirty, she still wasn't worried, although she was noticing how gray clouds had started to fill the sky. The forecast had changed to include a chance of light rain and she wished he'd call if for no other reason than to let her know his expected time of arrival. He had a cellphone, so he didn't have any excuse.

By five, her mood had darkened to match the deepening twilight. She'd spent the entire afternoon packing the children's clothing and toys with their help, and now they were fretting over their beloved uncle's absence. Courtney had suddenly refused to let go of her and Kyle never left her side except to run to the window and stare down the lane.

At six, a light drizzle started to fall. Lisa's anger turned into full-fledged worry, although she pretended otherwise. To appease the children she whipped up a cheese pizza from scratch, and kept the canned chili simmering on the stove for Simon. As she served her meal she couldn't stop her thoughts from drifting in an unwelcome direction.

Branson wasn't so far away that he couldn't have returned by now. The winding roads were treacherous in places and she hated to think he might have had an accident.

The doorbell rang and she jumped at the unexpected intrusion.

'I'll bet it's Unca Simon,' Kyle said before he slid off his chair and rushed to the door.

Lisa doubted if Simon would ring the bell. It had to be Eula May or Hank, stopping by to check on them. By the time she'd wiped Courtney's face, Kyle had returned.

His eyes were wide. 'A policeman wants to talk to you.'

Fear pierced her heart. She grabbed Courtney and carried her to the entryway where a sheriff's deputy stood, clutching his Smokey-the-Bear hat. His heavy coat was damp and his shoes were wet.

'What's wrong?' she asked, swallowing her panic.

'That's what I'm here to find out, ma'am,' the young man in blue said politely.

Lisa blinked in surprise. 'We're fine.'

'We had a report from a Dr Travers that he couldn't reach you by phone. He asked us to check to make sure you and the children were all right.'

She breathed a sigh of relief. Simon hadn't forgotten them. 'The phones must be out of order. I'll be right back.'

Sure enough, the kitchen phone had no dial tone.

'Maybe one of your extensions is off the hook,' the deputy suggested, glancing at the youngsters.

'It wasn't us,' Kyle said defensively.

Courtney removed her thumb from her mouth. 'We're not 'lowed to use the phone.'

'That's good to know,' Lisa said, 'but why don't we check them anyway?'

Kyle acted as a guide to locating each extension. Before

long they'd diagnosed the problem and reassembled in the entryway.

'I'll notify Dr Travers about your line being dead,' the officer said. 'He'll be relieved to hear it's a mechanical failure.'

Lisa smiled. A warm feeling began to glow inside her at the thought of Simon's concern. His action of calling in the local law enforcement shouldn't have surprised her. It was a typical response from a man who, by his own admission, looked after his own.

'Oh, and Dr Travers also asked me to pass along this message. He'll be here no later than eight,' the officer said as he positioned his hat on his head.

'Thank you. For checking on us and for the message.'

The deputy grinned. 'My pleasure, ma'am. Have a nice evening.'

'So is Unca Simon gonna get here soon?' Kyle demanded once they were alone.

Lisa glanced at the clock. 'In about an hour and a half,' she said. 'Plenty of time for you to take your baths. How about it?'

Courtney bobbed her head with her thumb still in her mouth while Kyle thundered up the stairs. Thirty minutes later, two freshly scrubbed children had started a vigil for their uncle in the living room.

They sat at opposite ends of the sofa in front of the window, their attention glued to the driveway. Courtney sat in a pretty blue nightgown with a matching velour robe and fuzzy yellow slippers on her feet. Kyle wore his Superman pajamas underneath a blue plaid bathrobe. Since he claimed not to like his bedroom slippers, he'd agreed to wear a pair of socks instead.

Knowing the next hour would pass slowly if she didn't do something to break the monotony, Lisa sat down on the piano bench. The sleek black lines of the instrument beckoned to her and she could hardly wait to hear the quality of its sound. Now was as good a time as any to indulge her passion.

She began to softly play Beethoven's '*Für Elise*'. Lost in the music as her fingers flew across the keys, she didn't notice that her small audience had crept next to her until she'd hit the final note.

'You're as good as Mommy.' Courtney removed her wrinkled thumb from her mouth only long enough to speak.

'Why, thank you, sweetie,' Lisa said, pleased by the praise. 'But I'm sure your mother is much better than I am.'

'She lets us sit next to her sometimes,' Kyle offered hopefully.

Lisa extended her arms. 'Then climb aboard. You know something? I'll bet you both have beautiful voices, like your mother. Shall we sing a few songs?'

Courtney pulled her thumb out of her mouth as she sat on Lisa's right. 'Christmas,' she ordered.

Lisa looked to Kyle, seated on her left. 'Is Christmas music OK with you?'

He nodded, his brown eyes wide with undisguised excitement over the upcoming holiday.

Lisa thought of something cheery. 'Why don't we start with ''Jingle Bells''?'

Halfway through 'Rudolph, the Red-Nosed Reindeer,' the front door burst open. 'Unca Simon!' the two shrieked as they slipped off the piano bench to run across the plush white carpeting.

Lisa hung back, instantly conscious of her bedraggled appearance. Between cooking, cleaning and searching through the dusty attic for suitcases, she was a mess. At the very least she should have combed her hair.

Oh, well, it was too late now. Besides, she was here to look after the children, not to impress Simon.

As she watched him remove his coat and respond in kind to Courtney's and Kyle's enthusiastic greetings, she realized she was seeing a new side to the quiet physician. She'd never pictured him as being demonstrative, but as he grabbed the two kids around their waists and lifted them with ease, she revised her opinion. Apparently he reserved his signs of affection for a select few.

Her unexpected desire to be in that small circle for longer than a few weeks bordered on being painful.

'Miss me?' he asked.

'Yes,' they screamed with delight.

Simon's gaze met Lisa's and she saw something spark in his eyes as he moved closer. 'You're OK.'

For a split second, before his expression lost its heat, she imagined him enfolding her in his embrace. 'Yes.'

'You're wet, Unca Simon,' Kyle announced.

'It's raining,' he patiently explained, lowering the boy to the floor.

Courtney grabbed his head with both hands and stuck her face in front of his. 'You were gone *all day*, Unca Simon.'

'I had a lot of business to tend to.' Simon cast a meaningful glance in Lisa's direction and she understood he'd fill in the details later. 'But I came as soon as I could.'

'We were worried about you,' Kyle added. 'Even Lisa.'

Feeling Simon's gaze, Lisa blushed under his scrutiny. To think she'd been transparent enough for a five-year-old to read. She shrugged. 'I didn't like the idea of you driving in icy road conditions.'

The curiosity in his eyes turned to surprise, then a cross between pleasure and amusement.

At that moment Courtney apparently felt she'd been ignored long enough. She pulled her thumb out of her mouth and lifted up her bangs. 'Feel my head. I'm better. Lisa says my temp'chure is all gone. Is Mommy better, too?'

Simon obeyed her dictate. 'Yes, but it will take longer for her to get completely well.'

'Then she's not going to heaven to be an angel, like Daddy?' Kyle asked.

His question brought a lump to Lisa's throat.

'Not at all,' Simon reassured the boy. 'In fact, she'll be home in time to see what Santa Claus brings.'

Courtney's mouth turned down and Kyle dug one big toe into the carpeting. 'I don't think Santa's coming this year,' he muttered. 'Mama didn't take us to see him when he came to town last week.'

Lisa's heart went out to them. Before she could utter any words of encouragement, Simon spoke.

'Santa's coming to Farmington,' he told the children. 'I'll make sure that you won't miss him. I promise.'

Kyle's eyes lit up. 'So we can make our Christmas lists?'

Simon smiled. 'How else will you remember what you want to tell Santa?'

'Oh, boy!' Kyle scrambled up the stairs.

'Lisa made pizza for dinner,' Courtney informed him.

Simon appeared impressed. 'Was it good?'

Courtney nodded.

'Did you save a piece for me?'

Courtney popped her thumb out of her mouth. 'Two pieces. Come see.' She pointed. 'Down.'

Simon released her and she tugged on his hand for him to follow her into the kitchen. Kyle returned with his tablet a few minutes later. He climbed into a chair across from his uncle while Simon ate with Courtney sitting on his lap.

His ease at holding the child touched Lisa's heart. Clearly, he visited his extended family often for them to be so comfortable around him. Yet in spite of the attention he paid the two children she noticed the slight droop to his broad shoulders and the tired set to his mouth.

Thank goodness it was too late to set out for Farmington this evening. After Simon's stressful day, he needed to rest before undertaking their three-hour journey home, especially under inclement winter weather conditions.

'I thought we could pack tonight and leave first thing in the morning,' he said after he'd pushed his empty dishes away.

Kyle lifted his head. 'We already packed.'

Simon appeared surprised. 'You did?'

Kyle nodded. 'Toys and clothes and everything.'

Simon looked at Lisa. 'I didn't expect you—'

She shrugged. 'It gave us something to do this afternoon. We spent our time tidying the house, catching up on the laundry and playing games. By the way, I remembered you told Eula May to forward the mail, but I cancelled the newspaper.'

An unreadable expression appeared on his face and she was afraid she'd overstepped her bounds. He'd asked for her to help, not take charge.

'There's plenty left for you to do, though,' she hastened to add.

He raised an eyebrow. 'Oh?'

'You get to figure out how to load all of this stuff in the car,' she said pertly. 'Once you see everything we set aside, you'll need an engineering degree to make it all fit.'

'You won't leave any of our stuff behind, will you, Unca Simon?' Kyle asked, a worried wrinkle appearing on his forehead.

'If you packed it, I'll take it,' he promised.

Lisa looked across the table and saw Courtney's head

nodding against her uncle's chest. 'She's asleep,' she mouthed.

He nodded. Tucking her against him, he slowly rose. 'Bedtime, Kyle.'

'But I'm not tired.'

'We're making an early start in the morning. I'm going to turn in myself,' Simon answered.

Kyle turned questioning eyes upon Lisa. 'Are *you* going to bed, too?'

'After I finish my chores.'

Kyle returned to his scribbles. 'I'll stay up as long as Lisa does.'

Lisa opened her mouth to correct him, then stopped herself. It was Simon's place to deal with Kyle's open defiance, not hers, but she was curious to see how he would handle the situation.

'Your bedtime is at eight,' Simon said firmly. 'It's a quarter past.'

'Aw, Unca Simon,' he whined. 'Can't I just—?'

'Go to bed like you always do,' Simon finished for him in a tone that brooked no arguments.

A frown settled on Kyle's face, but he rose. 'Eight o'clock is for babies like Courtney. ''Sides, it's Saturday. I always get to stay up past my bedtime on the weekends.'

'I know, but we're getting up early tomorrow so you can't sleep late.'

'I can sleep in the car.' Kyle sounded hopeful.

Lisa couldn't contain herself. 'And miss the games I have planned?' She added just the right note of horror to her voice before she sighed. 'Oh, well. I guess if you sleep through them, then Courtney will have all the fun.'

Kyle's eyes narrowed. 'Games? Like what?'

'If I tell you now, they won't be a surprise, will they?' she asked.

Kyle wasn't totally convinced. 'Are they cool games?'

Lisa pretended affront. 'We had fun today, didn't we?'

'Yeah.'

'Then we will tomorrow, too.' She crouched down to his level. 'How about a goodnight hug before your uncle tucks you in for the night?'

Kyle squeezed her tightly before he scampered from the room.

'I'll lock up when I'm finished,' she told Simon. 'See you in the morning.'

He nodded as he carefully balanced Courtney's limp form in his arms, then disappeared after Kyle.

It didn't take Lisa long to wash the few dishes Simon had used. Although she was tired, her mental picture of Simon removing his clothes and sprawling out on the bed she'd enjoyed drove all thoughts of sleep from her mind. She strolled into the living room and gravitated toward the piano.

Music had always been her refuge when she needed consolation, direction or just plain old comfort. Right now, her conflicting emotions about Simon needed sorting out.

She made a sudden decision. Aware of the three people upstairs who were trying to sleep, she carefully closed the pocket doors at each end of the living room before she sat on the piano bench and coaxed the opening strains of Beethoven's 'Moonlight Sonata' from the keys.

Given her growing feelings for her boss, sharing living quarters with him wasn't a wise idea, she decided. Luckily, by this time tomorrow she'd be safe in her own home and far away from the temptation he provided. The arrangement, complete with children, presented far too cozy a scene of domestic bliss.

Her role in his life was only temporary—he'd made that plain. Granted, she'd promised Patsy to help him for the next few weeks, but afterwards their relationship would return to the same well-defined boundaries of employer and employee.

Simon listened to Lisa's music as he stood in the doorway, hesitant to make his presence known. She certainly deserved some time to herself after spending the entire day entertaining two children. Then again, she might be glad to have an adult conversation for a change.

She sighed and he took it as his cue to enter. 'I didn't realize you played the piano.'

Her hands stilled. 'Everyone needs a hobby,' she said before an apology appeared on her face. 'Did I wake you?'

'Not at all. I wasn't ready for bed anyway, but I thought Kyle wouldn't dig his heels in so deep if he knew I was tired. Did they wear you out today?'

Her smile did funny things to him. 'You're forgetting my own nieces and nephews,' she answered. 'I was pleasantly surprised to see Kyle and Courtney accept me so easily. I'd expected more of a fight.'

'They've had several nannies and various babysitters over the years. They're used to new faces.'

'Lucky for me,' she said lightly. 'I had visions of both of them crying for their mom all day but, other than not letting me out of their sight, they did fine. Speaking of fine, how's Patsy?'

'I'm cautiously optimistic,' he said. 'Her recent alcohol problems apparently stem from depression over Mick's death. I sat in on one of their therapy sessions, so I'm hoping she'll pull herself together rather quickly.'

'I'm glad.'

'Sorry it took so long to drive back,' he began. 'It took time to organize Patsy's legal affairs with her attorney and business manager and to arrange for a press release.

Hopefully, our statement will keep the tabloid reporters off everyone's doorstep.'

A wrinkle appeared on Lisa's forehead. 'Do you think the news media will create a problem?'

'Who knows? But it's best to be prepared.'

She nodded, apparently agreeing with his philosophy. 'By the way, thanks for sending the cavalry to check on us.'

Simon leaned one hip against the piano, drinking in her appearance. Her short hair, usually neatly combed, now framed her face in wild abandon. She smelled like fresh bread and pizza sauce, probably because she wore a little of each on her gray tracksuit.

Those few stains confirmed the rightness of his decision to ask for her help. Lisa clearly placed a higher priority on the children's needs than on her personal appearance, which, to him, was as it should be.

'I was worried about you,' he said softly.

'The kids were fine.'

'I wasn't concerned about them.'

His gruff announcement startled her. 'You weren't?'

He shook his head. 'You were in a strange house, in a strange neighborhood. If you'd had an emergency, you didn't even know where Patsy kept her car keys.'

'I'm not totally inept.' Her glare could have singed holes in his knitted pullover. 'Nor was I born yesterday.'

Her tart remark amused him. 'I didn't mean to offend you. I don't like loose ends and I'd left several. That's all.'

'And your imagination took care of the rest.'

He hated to admit it. 'Yeah.'

She paused before a chagrined smile crossed her features. 'Don't feel too badly,' she said, her tone indulgent. 'My imagination got a little overactive, too. I was worried about *you*.'

'You were?' It had been a long time since someone had worried about him. In fact, he couldn't remember the last time it had happened. Patsy fretted over him from time to time in the way sisters did but, being family, she didn't count.

'I had you in everything from a five-car pile-up on the interstate to dropping into a ravine and we wouldn't find your body until spring,' she confessed.

He grinned. 'Spring, huh?'

'Right after the snow melted.'

'I, for one, am glad that I'm here and not stuck in a drift.' Simon grabbed her hand and pulled her into his loose embrace, focusing on her wide mouth and slightly parted lips. He faced more danger from internal flames of spontaneous combustion than from the external chill of a snowdrift.

His need to kiss her grew with each breath he took.

'Me, too,' she said, her voice slightly above a whisper.

The expectant look on her face, her refusal to pull away from him, were signs pointing in one direction… She wouldn't deny him what he wanted. Her stance and half-closed eyes proclaimed the wealth of passion hidden underneath Lisa's competent exterior.

A wealth of passion for him.

The situation reminded him of a starving man being offered his first sustaining meal in years—he couldn't resist. He didn't *want* to deny himself a taste of heaven.

He bent his head and lightly brushed his lips against hers. A hundred different sensations bombarded him, all revolving around Lisa's special scent, the feel of her body against his, the tangy taste of tomato on her lips, the aroma of oregano on her breath.

Simon pulled her closer until their bodies were pressed together. He ached with need and he let himself concentrate only on the woman in his arms at this moment, in this place.

Patsy's place.

Instant guilt flooded over him.

This shouldn't be happening. The timing was all wrong. He'd spent most of his life placing his sister's needs before his own. It would be cruel and heartless to carry on a romance underneath her nose while the loss of her husband still cut so deep. He faced months—if not longer—of giving whatever moral support was required to see her through this crisis. No woman, not even one with as generous a heart as Lisa, would accept a position of second place for an indefinite length of time.

He pulled away, knowing he had to say something to remove the dreamy look from her eyes. 'Thanks for being here for the kids,' he said, wincing at his repeated comment. 'I appreciate everything you've done.'

A look of puzzlement, then one of pain flashed across Lisa's face as she plainly understood his message. His kiss was one of gratitude and nothing else. An instant later her features returned to her professionally impassive lines. 'You're welcome.'

Everything about her—the stiffness in her voice, her straight spine—showed how completely he'd succeeded in bursting her bubble of happiness.

He felt like a complete jerk. She deserved an explanation, but before he could think of how and where to begin, something—some*one*—pounded on the door.

The unexpected intrusion drove everything else out of his mind. 'What the—?'

She shrugged. 'It's a little late for a social call.'

Simon strode across the room, conscious of Lisa following him. To his surprise, he found Eula May outside. Rain had plastered the woman's gray hair to her head and small ice crystals covered her coat.

'Please, you have to help me,' she begged, tears shimmering in her eyes as she wiped her nose. 'Hank's had an accident.'

CHAPTER SEVEN

Simon pulled his coat off the bannister where he'd thrown it and slid his arms through the sleeves. 'What happened?'

'He slipped on our porch. Hit the back of his head against the concrete step.'

'Did he lose consciousness?'

'Don't think so. He's cussin' up a storm, so I'm right sure he hasn't lost his senses, but he's bleedin' like a stuck hog.'

Lisa noticed the dark stains on Eula May's coat. At first she'd thought the rain had been responsible—now she knew otherwise.

'Where is he?' Simon asked.

'In the car. The phones are out or else I'd have called an ambulance. I thought maybe you could give him a look-see.' Eula May's voice cracked.

'The first-aid kit is upstairs,' Lisa said, remembering she'd seen it in the bathroom's medicine cabinet.

'We'll work in the kitchen.' Simon turned toward Eula May as he opened the door. 'Watch your step. We don't want two patients instead of one.'

Lisa found the kit and began setting up a makeshift doctor's office, hoping Hank's trauma wasn't too severe. With head injuries, one never knew.

Footsteps and voices warned her of their arrival. Simon hovered over Hank, gripping his elbow as he guided his latest patient through the doorway. 'Any dizziness?'

'Nah.' Hank's voice was strong in spite of his pasty-looking face. The blue handkerchief he pressed to the back of his head was liberally soaked with blood.

Lisa pulled out a chair for Hank and he sat, legs sprawled, while Eula May wrung her hands at his side.

'Quit fussing at me, Mother,' he scolded. 'I only cut open my head. I ain't dyin'.'

'That's for Doc Simon to find out, you old goat,' Eula May contradicted him. 'You just don't listen to me, now, do you? You had to go outside before I sprinkled the steps with the Ice Melt.'

'The steps weren't slick,' he muttered.

Lisa handed Simon a pair of latex gloves and began organizing gauze pads and disinfectant wipes. While Simon parted the man's hair and began examining the wound, Lisa stood next to him, ready to assist.

'Did you black out?' Simon asked.

'Saw a few stars, but those mighta been the real kind. I was flat on my back and staring up at the sky. With Eula May screeching like a chicken with its head chopped off, I couldn't have passed out even if'n I'd wanted to.'

'I wasn't carryin' on,' Eula May insisted. 'I thought you'd finally gone and done yourself in. But if the steps weren't slick, then what—?'

'Aw, hell, woman. You're gonna make me say it, ain't you? I wasn't wearing my dadburned glasses. Misjudged the distance and slid down like a marble in a chute.'

'Maybe now you'll wear 'em,' Eula May declared as she held Hank's hand in both of hers. 'Don't do you much good if they're in your shirt pocket.'

'See what I have to put up with, Doc?' Hank complained. 'She ain't never gonna let me have a minute's peace about those spectacles now.'

Lisa shared a glance with Simon. In spite of Hank's

grievances and his wife's scolding, their affection was obvious.

'I'm sure she'll forget in time,' Lisa said, handing Simon another clean gauze pad.

Hank winced as Simon gently cleaned the gash. 'Eula May's got the memory of an elephant.'

'Be glad, you old coot,' Eula May chided. 'If I didn't, you wouldn't remember what day of the week it was.'

'It's Saturday,' Hank snapped. 'Nigh on to ten o'clock, too. Now, Eula May, hush up so Simon can get on about his business of fixin' my head and we can get on home.'

'There isn't a lot of fixing I can do,' Simon apologized. 'The cut on your scalp needs about five stitches, but I don't have any sutures. When you go to the ER—'

'ER?' Hank roared. 'I don't need a hospital. I got a doctor right here.'

'Yes, but I also think you should have an MRI to check for skull fractures and stay in for observation. Concrete isn't very forgiving when it comes to the human body.'

'Dadburn it,' Hank muttered. 'I feel fine. Other than a grandaddy of a headache.'

Simon stepped around to stand in front of Hank while Lisa took his place to gently dab at the blood still trickling from the wound. 'What about nausea or vomiting?'

'My stomach's upset some but, then, Eula May fixed—'

Hank's wife shook her finger in his face. 'Don't you dare make one peep about my cooking, Hank Willson. I told you that I was tryin' out a new recipe for supper. I had no idea it would turn out so spicy.'

'I'll say.' Hank leaned closer to Simon. 'Damn near had to eat a whole bottle of Rolaids. I'll be having stomach troubles from now till Christmas.'

Eula May sniffed. 'Have you all noticed who's doing the fussin'? It sure isn't me.'

Lisa grinned, wondering if the two squabbled all the time.

Simon rummaged through a drawer near the sink, pulled out a small flashlight and proceeded to check Hank's pupils. 'Any double vision?'

'Nah.' As Simon clicked off the light, Hank asked, 'What's the verdict?'

'I'd feel better if we could run a few tests, but I'm afraid you have a slight concussion.'

'Should I drive him to the hospital?' Eula May asked.

Hank groaned. 'Now, Mother. A concussion is just a fancy way to say my brains got shook. I'll get over it.'

'If it were my spouse,' Simon said slowly, 'I'd bundle her in the car and be on my way.'

Lisa thought he would. If he'd ask the sheriff to check on a potential threat to his family, he wouldn't dally over a real one.

Hank crossed his arms. 'And if'n I don't want to go?'

Simon shrugged as he stripped off his gloves. 'I can't force you. Odds are, you'll be fine on your own. Your wife, however, will probably worry herself sick. You might prepare yourself for her to ask every five minutes how you're feeling.'

Hank's face puckered into a frown. 'It won't be askin'. It'll be *houndin'*. Have you ever seen a woman henpeck as much as Eula May?'

Simon appeared amused. 'She's concerned about you,' he corrected, clearly taking the middle ground. 'Whatever you decide to do, keep in mind that you'll probably suffer some after-effects. We've already talked about a headache and nausea, but you could notice some memory loss—'

Eula May interrupted, 'You mean worse than usual?'

Simon continued, 'A loss of co-ordination, numbness and possible ringing in the ears.'

Eula May gasped. 'Land sakes. He don't hear me now half the time. I'd hate to think of him having more ear troubles.'

Hank winked at Lisa and she returned his smile. Obviously Hank suffered from selective hearing from time to time. Her father had the same ailment.

'You might even develop seizures,' Simon added. 'It wouldn't be so bad if the phones were working because she could call the ambulance. But as they are now, you could be flirting with danger…' He shrugged, letting Hank fill in the blank.

'Hank Willson. You're gettin' in the car right now and that's final,' Eula May declared. 'If I'm gonna lose sleep, frettin' over you, I'd rather do my frettin' in the hospital.'

'Oh, all right,' Hank muttered. 'I won't get a minute's peace otherwise.'

'To be on the safe side,' Simon said, 'I'll go along to keep you both company.'

Lisa didn't get a chance to voice an opinion one way or the other. Simon ushered Hank and Eula May to the door before she could squeak out a farewell and wish them good luck.

Either Simon was more concerned about Hank than he'd let on, or he was simply eager to stay as far away from her as possible. As the silence descended upon the house, she suspected it was the latter.

True, Hank needed X-rays. Knowing Simon as she did, he would also worry about the elderly couple travelling on the potentially hazardous roads.

However, had the neighbours not interrupted them, they would have both scattered to opposite ends of the house, like boxers going to their corners to tend their wounds.

She'd been such a fool for not resisting his gentle tug. She also should have shown more restraint when he'd kissed her, instead of taking his gesture as a sign of interest. As she thought about the way she'd leaned against him, flung her arms around his neck and toyed with the neckline of his sweater, an embarrassed heat surged through her entire body.

For whatever reason, her actions and what they revealed about her innermost thoughts had clearly scared him to the point where he'd run for the proverbial hills.

Rejection took such a long time to heal. At least this time Simon's rebuff had come before she'd totally lost her head and started thinking of orange blossom and white satin.

She didn't deny that he was a handsome man. And, yes, she was attracted to him against her better judgement. Now that she could think calmly about the incident, the cause of her strong and uninhibited responses became obvious.

Stress was the culprit. The upcoming holiday, worrying about Simon's gift, thinking about her cruise, proving that Bryan was only a dim memory to her—these were making her a little crazy. Her knees would probably go just as weak if another guy had kissed her.

A tropical vacation was exactly what she needed to work these ridiculous urges out of her system and regain her perspective.

In the meantime, she would do well to remember the two things Simon wanted from her—one, to help with the children and, two, to be an efficient nurse. Nothing more, nothing less. Falling in love with him wasn't part of his—or her—plan.

Pushing aside all thoughts of Simon Travers, she tiptoed upstairs to check on the children and take a shower. Unfortunately, the bar of soap she used smelled exactly like him, and she wondered if she should stay awake until he returned.

No, she decided. If she did, it would be an awkward moment for both of them. Also, she could easily have to wait for hours. They faced a busy day tomorrow and one adult had to be fresh enough to meet the challenges of installing two children in their temporary home away from home. That being her job, she should get some sleep.

On the other hand, she wanted to show how quickly and completely she'd forgotten the piano incident. She intended to act as if their kiss had meant as little to her as it apparently had to him.

Her promise to Patsy weighed heavily on her. Simon plainly preferred to handle his personal life on his own, and after tonight she would rather keep her distance.

Maybe it was possible for her to fulfil her moral obligation and steer clear of Simon, too. She would simply take the children with her several nights a week, freeing Simon to swim to his heart's content. After five o'clock and the clinic closed, their paths wouldn't have to cross. Divorced households managed with a similar plan—it should also work for them.

Lisa checked on the children one last time before she claimed the master bedroom for the night. It was nearer to the children than the guest room and also would allow her to hear Simon's return even if she didn't welcome him home.

She had just turned on the table lamp and crawled into bed with another magazine—a gourmet cooking one this time—when she heard the distant warble of a bell.

It sounded like a phone, but the one beside the bed remained silent.

The noise came again. Lisa flung back the covers and started her search, closing the children's doors before she flicked on the lights. The ring grew louder as she approached the steps and she followed it to the lower level.

She rushed into the living room where, surprisingly, the sound lost its intensity. Backtracking to the entryway, she narrowed the direction down. The melodic ring seemed to be coming from inside the tall vase standing on the floor next to the bottom step. No wonder she'd overlooked it on her first trip through.

She peeked inside and found a cellphone. Simon's, no doubt. Quickly, she punched a button, hoping the caller hadn't given up. 'Hello.'

'Lisa.' Simon's voice sounded relieved. 'I'd noticed my phone was missing from my coat pocket. I was hoping it was still in the house.'

'It had fallen in the vase,' she said, pleased because her voice sounded so crisp and professional though her heart pounded a mile a minute. Suddenly she was afraid he was calling with bad news. 'How's Hank?'

'His tests turned out OK. We're on our way back. As soon as he's settled, I'll be home.'

His reference to 'home' was bitter-sweet and she swallowed the knot in her throat. 'I'll leave the door unlocked.'

'No!' he shouted in her ear. 'Don't. I have a spare key with me.'

'Fine,' she snapped, irritated over his rejection of what she considered a kind act. 'I'll see you in the morning.'

His voice became apologetic. 'I didn't mean to yell. It's just that the house is fairly remote. I want you to be safe.'

She assumed his use of 'you' had been offered in the plural and not the singular sense. Because the house *was* in a remote location, she'd considered her offer a reasonable one, but he clearly didn't see the situation in the same way she did.

'OK. I'll lock the door.'

'I'll see you in the morning,' he said.

'Goodnight.' Lisa hit the 'End' button. Another twenty-four hours in Simon's presence. By this time tomorrow, Courtney and Kyle would be settled in Simon's house and she would be in hers.

Then, as of Monday morning, she would fall back into her professional mode and think of Simon as her boss rather than a caring uncle. Other than asking about Courtney and Kyle, personal topics would once again be off limits and they would go their somewhat separate ways.

Don't forget his Christmas present.

No problem, she decided. On those nights when she entertained the children, she could grill them for ideas.

Everything was going to work out perfectly.

Simon glared at her on Monday morning as he guided his two charges toward his office. Each child carried a brand-new coloring book and box of crayons.

'I want to know what you did to these kids,' he muttered in her ear.

Lisa stared at him in surprise. 'What are you talking about?'

'Hi, Lisa,' Courtney and Kyle greeted her. 'We're going to help Unca Simon work.'

Lisa glanced at Simon, noticing that his expression resembled a thundercloud. 'You are?'

'Wait in my office, will you, please?' Simon asked the children.

Courtney and Kyle disappeared, presumably to entertain themselves with their colouring books. Simon grabbed Lisa by the arm and steered her toward the privacy of their tiny lab.

'What do you mean, what did I do to the kids?' she asked. 'You were with me the whole time.'

'You must have done something,' he insisted. 'Because, not an hour after you left, their personalities changed.'

She held up her hands, like a cop directing traffic. 'Hold on. What are you saying?'

'Your exhaust fumes hadn't even cleared the air before those two turned into the Grumpy Twins.'

Lisa grinned. Her sister voiced the same complaint about her husband. Whenever he left, her two angels became hellions.

'They're upset by all the changes. Give them time to settle in.'

'I understand that, but why do they "settle in" for you and not for me? I never had any problems before,' he said accusingly. 'What did you *do* to them?'

'Nothing. Honest. I just loved them,' she said simply.

He finger-combed his hair, giving it a windblown appearance. 'For some reason, I couldn't do anything right.'

'All you had to do was read them a story and tuck them into their new beds.'

Simon crossed his arms. 'I apparently didn't accomplish either to their satisfaction. All I heard was how Lisa turned the pages *this* way and how Lisa pulled the covers over them *that* way.'

She grinned.

'When Courtney woke up in the night with a nightmare, she wanted to cuddle with you instead of me because you could sing to her. I ended up humming "Row Your Boat" for thirty minutes because I couldn't think of the words *or* another song.'

Lisa burst out laughing, then covered her mouth at his stormy expression. He wasn't amused by her humour at his expense. 'I'm sorry,' she choked out.

'It wouldn't have been so bad, but Courtney informed me that I can't carry a tune in a bucket.'

'Oh, Simon,' Lisa chided. 'You know children at that age are refreshingly honest. Don't take it so hard.'

'I'm not upset over the bucket comment. I'm fully aware of how Patsy received all the musical ability in the family. What bothers me is how everything I do falls short of what *you* do.'

'Now, Simon. That's not true and you know it. If it's any consolation, they ran me through the same hoops on Saturday.'

He didn't appear convinced. 'It's a sad day when a man can't even slap cereal on the table without the kids finding fault,' he grumbled.

'What did you give them?' she asked. 'Something really healthy, I suppose. High in fiber and low in sugar content, right?'

'I happen to enjoy granola,' he defended himself.

'Yeah, well, you'd better stop at the grocery store tonight and buy the brands they'll eat.'

After their arrival in Farmington on Sunday afternoon, they'd prioritized their needs. Sleeping arrangements had topped the list, so they'd shopped for twin beds and the necessary linen. By the time everything had been delivered, the frames assembled in Simon's spare room and the beds made with brand-new sheets and blankets, the day had been nearly gone.

She'd volunteered to run after groceries, but he'd insisted on saving that errand for today.

'You didn't let them go hungry, did you?'

He shot her a disgusted frown. 'Absolutely not. They ate it, but with the stipulation of letting them pour their own servings. Apparently you'd told them they were old enough to do it for themselves.'

'What's wrong with that? They need to become independent.'

He raised one eyebrow. 'They dumped three-fourths of

the box on the table. I also couldn't pour their milk for the same reason.'

Lisa cringed, picturing the two struggling with a gallon milk jug.

'They wanted a small pitcher, but my measuring cup wouldn't do. I had to borrow a creamer from the neighbor.'

Lisa pictured Simon knocking on the Holdens' door and asking for a creamer. She pressed her lips together and covered her mouth to hide her mirth.

'Then,' he continued to list his grievances, 'neither of them wanted to change out of their pajamas because *you* let them wear theirs all day on Saturday.'

Lisa winced. Since Courtney had been sick, the only way she'd been able to encourage her to stay in bed had been to let her wear her nightie. Kyle, not to be slighted, had been allowed the same privilege.

'They're dressed now,' she pointed out.

'Only because they were afraid that if they came here someone would think they were sick and give them a shot.'

Lisa was aghast. 'Did you threaten them?'

'I did not.' Simon's affront was obvious as he empha-sized each word. 'I calmly mentioned that children who wore their nightclothes to the doctor's office were usually ill. Kyle assumed the rest.'

He drew a deep breath, as if fortifying himself. 'I know we agreed on you watching the kids three nights a week, but I think we should be more flexible.'

'More flexible?' she echoed. 'How?'

Courtney appeared in the doorway. 'Did you ask her yet, Unca Simon?'

The aggrieved tone he'd been using suddenly changed to an indulgent one. 'Not yet.'

Courtney planted her hands on both hips. 'Well,' she demanded, 'hurry up and ask her.'

'I will. After you go back to my office,' Simon said.

As soon as Courtney had flounced away, Lisa met Simon's troubled gaze. 'Ask me what?'

'The kids want to know if you'll join us on some of the other evenings, too. For activities like skating, movies, going to see Santa—that sort of thing.'

His request had put her in a hard spot. She hated to refuse and hated to spend time with Simon. Lisa leaned against the counter and rubbed the back of her neck.

'I know you have a life of your own,' Simon said, 'but if you could come along, at least for a little while, they'd appreciate it.'

Lisa drew a deep breath. Maintaining a businesslike demeanor toward Simon was possible while she was at work because she could focus her attention on patients and medical issues. Being on his home turf was another matter.

Unless, of course, he wanted her there.

'What do *you* want, Simon?'

Although he hesitated before answering, his gaze didn't waver. 'I want to make the kids happy.'

If she'd ever needed confirmation that Simon would put the needs of his family before his own, this was it. He'd literally run away after their kiss and didn't want to spend time with her now. Keeping her distance was a crucial part in stifling her attraction to Simon, but she didn't want to disappoint the children either.

'I'll try,' she conceded. 'But I can't promise.'

Courtney rushed in and tugged on his coatsleeve. 'Did you ask her? Can she come with us?'

'Hang on a minute, Court,' he said patiently.

Lisa crouched down to the little girl's eye level. For all of Simon's complaints, he'd done a good job of dressing Courtney. Her socks matched her green long-sleeved sweatshirt and her ponytail hung only slightly off-center.

'What do you want to ask me?'

'Will you go with us to the grocery store tonight?' Courtney leaned closer and cupped her hand over her mouth to speak in Lisa's ear. However, her whisper was loud enough for everyone to hear. 'Unca Simon don't have much to eat in his house.'

Lisa ruffled Courtney's bangs. 'I'm sure your uncle will fill his cupboards with your favorite food. You'll have to tell him exactly what you want.'

'Please, won't you come wif us?'

'I'd love to, but I can't. Not tonight.'

Courtney glanced at Simon, her lower lip trembling, before she looked back at Lisa. 'Why not?'

'Because I'm going to my mother's house. It's her birthday.'

'My friend, Lucy, had a clown at her party. He did tricks and threw stuff in the air and everything.' Courtney raised her arms to demonstrate.

Lisa rose. 'No clown. Just my parents, my brothers, my sister and their families.' Knowing her younger brother's love of practical jokes, he could easily be considered the family clown.

Courtney's bright face dimmed and she spoke wistfully, 'Cake and ice cream.'

'I imagine.'

'We're gonna have s'getti out of a can. Unca Simon said so.' If the little girl's spirits drooped any more, she'd be stepping on them.

Lisa glanced at Simon. '*Canned* spaghetti?'

He shrugged. 'They requested it.'

She knew she would regret what she was about to do, but she couldn't stop herself. Glancing down at Courtney, she asked, 'Would you like to come to the party with me? You, Kyle and…your uncle?'

Courtney's countenance radiated excitement. 'Can we?'

Lisa glanced at Simon and raised one eyebrow in silent query. If he wanted to decline, now was the time to say so.

He offered a small smile and a faint nod. 'If that's how you want to spend your evening…'

'Yippee!' Courtney screeched before she ran from the room, shouting at the top of her lungs. 'Guess what, Kyle? We's goin' to a birfday party wif Lisa.'

'If crashing your family gathering is a problem…' Simon began.

'Not at all,' Lisa said. 'It's my mom's sixty-fifth, so we've invited a lot of my parents' friends and neighbours. No one will notice a few more people. Because I'm organizing things beforehand, I don't have time to go with you to the store.'

'We'll manage.' He grinned. 'Now, if I can find a sitter for the kids, my day will be complete. I'd hoped the hospital's center would take them, but they're full. I don't know who else to call. Any suggestions?'

She immediately thought of her sister, but hated the thought of one more tie between herself and Simon. However, the children's welfare came first. While having them in the clinic this morning wasn't a problem, staying in Simon's office wasn't a suitable long-term solution.

'My sister watches two children in addition to her own kids,' Lisa said slowly. 'She might be able to watch Courtney and Kyle for a few weeks.'

Simon's eyes lit up. 'Do you think so? Could she take them today? Right now?'

'I'll find out.' Lisa punched her sister's number into the wall phone's keypad and, at Jill's answering hello, explained Simon's dilemma without going into great detail.

'I'll be happy to look after them,' Jill replied. 'Is this Simon the sexy doctor you work for?'

Conscious of Simon standing nearby, Lisa managed a smile and hoped he couldn't overhear her conversation. 'Yeah.'

'If you'd like, I'm about to run errands. I can pick them up at the clinic.'

Patients were already waiting, so Lisa made the decision. 'That would be wonderful. See you in a few minutes.'

She replaced the receiver. 'Jill's leaving to run an errand. She'll pick up Courtney and Kyle on her way home.'

Simon's eyes sparkled with new life and he grabbed her by the shoulders. 'You're a lifesaver.' In the next breath, he bent his head and planted a hard, swift kiss on her mouth. 'Thanks.'

He hurried away, leaving Lisa in a state of numbed shock before anger took hold. She didn't want his kiss of gratitude, which was what Saturday's and now today's had been. She wanted a kiss of passion, of love—a kiss where she consumed his every thought.

He could save his appreciative, superficial pecks for little old ladies. And she intended to tell him so at the next available opportunity.

CHAPTER EIGHT

BETWEEN the usual Monday morning rush of scheduled patients and those who'd succumbed to the latest virus, Lisa felt as if she barely had time to breathe, much less think.

The waiting room had filled to a capacity crowd, so she only took a few minutes to quickly introduce Simon and Jill, hug the children goodbye and promise to see them later. For the next three hours, she herded people in and out of the five waiting rooms so that Simon could go from one case to another without any delay. Respiratory complaints topped the list, which wasn't surprising for this time of year.

As noon approached, her stack of folders slowly dwindled to three.

'Andrea Brooks,' she announced.

Yvonne Brooks ushered her brood forward. 'I'm sorry to bring everyone again. But you know how it is.'

'It's OK. We don't mind.'

Yvonne sighed. 'Last week it was Holly. This week it's Andrea. I suppose next week it will be Troy. Worse yet, it could be me.'

Lisa led the small group into an exam room. While three-year-old Holly appeared much improved since the last visit, five-year-old Andrea didn't. Her face was flushed and her eyes appeared dull. Lisa couldn't help but compare the health of these youngsters to that of Simon's robust niece and nephew.

'Is your throat sore?' Lisa asked the little girl.

Andrea nodded and wiped the back of her hand across her eyes. Her lower lip quivered.

'Same symptoms Holly had.' Yvonne sounded defeated. 'If they were going to get sick, I wish they'd be sick together.'

'Most mothers would agree. Unfortunately, it doesn't work that way.'

'I know. I can't wait until one of them brings home chickenpox. I'll fight that for weeks.'

Lisa recorded Andrea's temperature. As she'd expected, it was elevated. 'She's probably caught Holly's bug. We'll see what Dr Travers says.'

Leaving the room, she dropped the chart in the wall bin by the door, indicating that the patient was ready to be seen. She returned to the waiting room and called the next name.

'Helena Vogel.'

The sixty-two-year-old widow greeted her with a huge smile. 'Hello, dearie. How's my favourite neighbour?'

Lisa smiled at the woman who lived three houses away from hers and was as active as a person half her age. 'I'm fine. How about you?'

'I'm here for my flu shot. Time just slipped away from me and I told myself to get here before it was too late.'

'You're in luck. I have several doses left.' Lisa showed Helena to another room. 'Have a seat and I'll be right back.'

She returned a few minutes later with a filled syringe in hand. 'Are you ready?'

Helena rolled up her sleeve. 'Aw, dearie, I'm always ready. Ready for anything. And speaking of being ready, a little bird has told me that you're going on a cruise in a few weeks.'

'That's right.' Lisa gave her the injection.

Helena sighed. 'Oh, my, I love cruises. I've taken one

every year for the last five years. Went to Alaska this past summer.' She patted Lisa's arm. 'Had a ball. You will, too.'

'I'm sure I will.'

'Take lots of pictures.' Helena winked. 'The beach has such marvelous beefcake strutting about.'

'Mrs Vogel!'

'Now, now. All of my urges haven't totally dried up with the rest of me.' Helena's eyes twinkled. 'Are you going with anyone I know?'

Lisa grinned, aware of Helena's fishing expedition. 'Savanna Gibson. You've met her. She's Dr Foster's nurse.'

'My, yes. I know Savanna. Lovely girl. Very outgoing. Tell me, is this a singles' cruise?'

'I don't know.' Savanna had never said but, knowing of her friend's interest in eligible males, Lisa wouldn't be surprised.

Helena gave a theatrical sigh. 'Two young women on the prowl. Oh, to be your age again.'

'I'm not sure I'd say we're on the prowl,' Lisa demurred.

'You're out for a good time, aren't you?' Helena demanded.

'Well, yes, but—'

'Did I ever tell you about a gentleman I met when I sailed to Nassau some years ago?'

Lisa felt as if she'd been caught up in a whirlwind. 'No.'

Helena closed her eyes in apparent rapture over the memory. 'He was a dream. Rich, handsome and, oh, how he could tango.'

'Really?' She didn't have any trouble imagining the spry Helena gliding across a dance floor in stiletto heels.

'He was a fantastic kisser and, oh, how he could make a girl…' She grinned as she rose. 'Never mind. I'd better run. I'm meeting Clyde at the Senior Center for lunch.' In the next instant she was gone, leaving a trace of her lavender fragrance in the air.

Lisa wished she could have met the energetic Helena thirty years ago. She'd probably given a number of men a run for their money.

She went to call the next patient and ran into Simon as he came out of Andrea Brooks's room.

'Give her a bicillin injection,' he ordered, handing her the chart. 'Looks like tonsillitis is going around the family.'

'Do you want a culture for strep?'

He pursed his mouth in thought. 'Holly's was negative, so I doubt if Andrea's will be different. Even so, better go ahead to be on the safe side.'

'I don't mean to question you, but is it really necessary?' Lisa's challenge startled him and she hurried to add, 'Money is so tight for them right now. Yvonne doesn't have anyone to help her.'

'A bout with rheumatic fever won't be less expensive.'

'I know it won't, but you *are* treating her…' Her voice faded. Rheumatic fever was a complication from an undiagnosed and untreated Group A strep infection.

'I want the culture.' He emphasized each word.

'OK. Just thought I'd ask.'

He turned away, then hesitated. 'Can we absorb the cost of one strep test?'

Reading between the lines, Lisa bestowed a huge smile on him. 'Yes.'

Simon stepped toward the next door and pulled the chart from the wire holder on the wall. 'Then arrange it.'

'I will.' Thanks seemed in order, but she hesitated. Simon wasn't the type who'd appreciate praise for performing a nice gesture.

He glanced up from reviewing the notes pinned to the chart in his hand. 'Did you need something else?'

His comment pulled her out of her reverie. 'No. That is, you really are a kind-hearted man, aren't you?'

He gave her a lopsided smile. 'Yeah, but don't tell anyone. I don't want to ruin my image for the staff.' He turned the doorknob, then stepped inside to greet his next patient.

Lisa quickly swabbed Andrea's throat and gave her the antibiotic injection. She marked off the charges on the billing form Yvonne would present to the receptionist on her way out. The amount wasn't a lot, but when one didn't have the money even a small saving helped.

In fact, each year at Christmas time the clinic staff donated to a needy family and Lisa decided to submit the Brookses' names to Alice for consideration as possible recipients.

With that thought in mind she called her last patient, recognizing him as one of their asthma patients. 'Curt Norwood.'

A lanky redhead came forward and she smiled at him. 'Hi, Curt. How's it going today?'

'Not so good,' the twenty-year-old said before he broke into a coughing spasm. 'I'm having trouble breathing.'

Lisa heard a distinct wheeze as she guided him to a room. 'How long have you been like this?'

'It started about a week ago,' he said. 'I caught a cold and then it gradually got worse.'

'Are you using your inhaler?' she asked as she took his vital signs, noting his low-grade fever and slightly elevated blood pressure.

He nodded. 'Every four hours. This morning, though, I could tell it wasn't helping. I thought I'd see what Doc Simon has to say.'

'Good idea. He'll be in shortly.' She left the room and found Simon in the lab, scribbling on a chart.

He raised his head as she entered. 'All done?'

'Not quite,' she told him. 'Curt Norwood is here. Room two.'

Simon exchanged charts with her. 'His asthma?'

'He's wheezing quite a bit and has a temp,' she reported. Simon left and she took advantage of her spare moment to call her mother.

'I'm bringing a few extra guests,' Lisa announced. 'I hope it's OK.'

'Why, of course, dear. You should know better than to ask,' Rhonda Mallory chided. 'Anyone we know?'

'No, not really. It's Dr Travers and his niece and nephew. They're staying with him for a few weeks while his sister is—' Although she knew her mother wouldn't betray a confidence, she didn't feel she should discuss the specific details without Simon's permission. 'She's dealing with some personal problems right now.'

'I see.'

'Yeah, well, warn everybody to lay off the third degree. Simon likes his privacy.'

'Making conversation isn't giving the third degree,' Rhonda chided.

'Just don't push him for a lot of details, OK? I know how nosy our family can get. Although if you can help me on some Christmas ideas for him I'd appreciate it. The clinic staff voted me to be in charge of his gift and I'm drawing a complete blank.'

'For me to learn what would be an appropriate gift, I'm going to have to ask personal questions.'

'You know what I mean,' Lisa said, realizing how she'd contradicted herself.

Rhonda chuckled. 'I'll see what I can come up with for your Dr Travers.'

'He's not *my* Dr Travers,' Lisa corrected. 'He's my boss.'

'Whatever, dear.'

'He is,' she insisted.

'Yes, dear. See you at six.'

Lisa replaced the receiver and wondered why her mother had been humouring her. Her brother brought his dates to family functions all the time and no one thought twice about it. She deserved the same courtesy.

Simon stuck his head around the door. 'Curt has pneumonia and I've sent him down to Radiology for pictures. Let me know the minute they're through with him.'

'I will.'

'Do you think the kids are getting along OK with your sister?'

He sounded like a parent who'd left his child with a sitter for the first time. 'I'm sure they are, but you can drop by and see for yourself.'

He appeared pensive. 'Maybe I'll call. I'd hate to disrupt your sister's routine.'

Lisa laughed. 'My sister doesn't have a routine, although she serves lunch promptly at eleven-thirty.' She glanced at the clock. 'It's a quarter past twelve. They're probably getting ready for naps.'

SueEllen's voice came over the intercom. 'Dr Travers, line three.'

Simon headed for his office, leaving Lisa to unpack the latest shipment of supplies and replenish her cupboards with necessities like paper gowns, syringes and gauze.

Before long, Curt returned with his X-rays. Lisa had seen enough pictures to recognize the shadows around his bronchi.

'Lisa will give you an injection of an extremely powerful antibiotic called Rocephin,' Simon told him. 'I want you to come back tomorrow for a second dose.'

Curt nodded.

'In the meantime, do you have a pulmonary machine at home? If you don't, I'm going to admit you for respiratory therapy treatments.'

'I have one,' Curt assured him. 'I got it when I was a kid.'

'Then you know the routine. Albuterol solution in three ccs of saline. Inhale the mist until you've used the entire amount.'

'Yes, sir.'

'Don't forget, come back tomorrow. And either call me or go to the emergency room if you feel you're getting worse.'

'I will.'

Lisa carried out his orders, sent some samples of a decongestant with Curt, then eagerly went to lunch. Her blueberry muffin at breakfast had long disappeared and her stomach was demanding attention.

'Where *were* you all weekend?' Savanna asked as soon as Lisa entered the lounge.

So much for no one discovering her absence. 'Out of town.'

'Where did you go?'

They were alone, but Lisa lowered her voice anyway. 'I went with Si—Dr Travers this weekend.'

The other nurse's eyes nearly popped out of her head. 'Why, you sly thing, you. You really *do* have a thing going with our eligible Dr Travers.'

Lisa popped her frozen dinner into the microwave and set the timer. 'No, I don't. He had to bring his niece and nephew back with him and he asked me to go along.'

'Wow! Was this a one-nighter or two?' she asked slyly.

'It was two, but nothing happened,' Lisa hastened to add, although it hadn't been for a lack of willingness on her part. 'We were with his family the whole time.'

'Moving fast, aren't we?'

'Simon isn't interested in me one iota. Anyone would have done. I happened to be the only person he could find to tag along on short notice.' Lisa hid her disappointment behind a light tone and willed the microwave to hurry.

'Yeah right.' Savanna nibbled on her apple. 'And to think I called your mother to ask where you were.'

'You didn't.' Lisa was horrified.

'I did. Sorry.'

Lisa rubbed her forehead, feeling the tension build. No wonder her mother didn't believe her story about Simon being only a friend. Maybe she should arrive earlier than everyone else and explain—*really* explain—the situation between Simon and herself.

'So, what did you two do exactly?' Savanna asked.

Lisa glossed over the details. 'Simon had personal business with his sister, so I babysat on Saturday. We drove home on Sunday, fixed up a room for Courtney and Kyle— she's three and Kyle's five—and I went home. End of weekend.'

'Did you get any Christmas ideas for Dr Secretive while you were with him?'

The microwave beeped and Lisa removed her lunch. 'Not really.'

Savanna stared at her with an incredulous expression on her face. 'You spent an entire weekend with the man and didn't come up with any ideas?'

Lisa shrugged. 'So sue me.'

Savanna shook her head and clicked her tongue. 'Lisa, Lisa, Lisa. What am I going to do with you?'

'The same thing everyone else does,' she replied pertly. 'Nothing.'

'Haven't I told you to make the most of your opportunities? You had a golden one fall right into your lap.'

'OK. I screwed up. I'll have other chances.'

'When?'

'When I take the children shopping,' she said. 'I'm sure they'll give me some suggestions.'

Savanna started laughing. 'From a three-year-old and a five-year-old? Get serious.'

'Hey, my sister's kids are regular founts of knowledge,' Lisa protested. 'They repeat everything they hear.'

'Kids have an innate sense of knowing what's juicy gossip and what isn't. They remember the embarrassing things, word for word.'

'We'll do fine.'

'I still wouldn't bet the farm on them having reliable input,' Savanna cautioned.

'I won't. I'll be in and out of Simon's house to pick them up for our excursions so I'll keep my eyes open. I also have a secret weapon.'

'Oh, yeah?'

Lisa nodded. 'My mother.'

'And when are you going to pull her out of your magic hat? The day before the party?'

'Tonight,' Lisa mentioned. 'I felt so bad about the kids not having a decent meal, I invited them to join us for my mom's birthday party.'

Savanna stared at her, incredulous. 'You've just spent a weekend with him and his family and now you're introducing him to *your* parents? Do you realize what people will think? What they'll say?'

Considering how she hadn't been able to convince her own mother of their above-board relationship, she could easily imagine everyone else's conclusions.

'They'll see that we're only friends and colleagues. Nothing more.'

'Dream on.'

However, as Lisa got ready for the evening, she contemplated a strategy to counteract any false assumptions her family might make. Persuasion was out—no one would believe her.

Silence was her best plan. Without hand-holding, stolen kisses and secret smiles, her mother would see that Simon was simply a colleague. She'd hidden her attraction for him these past six months—a few more weeks would be as easy as signing her own name.

Shortly before six o'clock, Simon arrived at her apartment. With the children's help, they loaded his car with her contributions to the party and headed for the Mallory homestead on the edge of town. The house itself stood near the back of a double lot and the long driveway led to an unattached two-car garage on the west side.

Lisa pulled next to the steel building. 'My dad tinkers with car engines and spends a lot of time out here. A few years ago he installed a heater so he could work year round.'

Simon slid out from behind the wheel and surveyed the surroundings. 'Is he a mechanic?'

'He was before he retired from the county. He worked in their machine shop. Now cars are his hobby.' She handed Kyle a grocery sack of buns and Courtney a bag of potato chips to carry.

'I think Mom plans her huge parties just so he'll be forced to clean the garage out from time to time.'

Simon grinned. 'A sneaky manoeuvre.'

'Yeah, but it's effective.'

She walked to the regular-sized door, balancing two large bowls of pasta salad while Simon carried in a crockpot of baked beans. Inside the garage, she threaded her way around the tables and chairs for the guests to the far east end where her mother stood by the long counter she'd commissioned to hold the food.

Lisa performed the introductions, carefully treating Simon as any other old friend before she steered the children to the play area in one corner.

'It looks great in here,' she said as soon as Kyle and Courtney were occupied. The haphazard array of tools and car parts had been tidied and the concrete floor swept clean. The wall heater blew forth a steady stream of warm air and the entire room was comfortable, in spite of the freezing temperatures outside.

Rhonda smiled. Her blonde hair and trim figure camouflaged her age. Lisa envied her ability to wear even the most casual attire—in this case, a navy blue windsuit—and appear elegant.

'Your father's worked hard for the last two days. I tried to help him, but he wouldn't let me.'

'How thoughtful,' Lisa said, touched by her father's gesture.

Rhonda's look was one of exasperation. 'Hardly. Apparently, I couldn't clean his precious work space to his satisfaction.'

'Now, Ronnie,' Richard Mallory said as he approached, wearing what Lisa recognized as his standard winter attire of a flannel shirt and jeans. His hair always had an unkempt look, which drove her mother to distraction. 'Let's not give our guest the wrong impression.'

Richard shook Simon's hand. 'My wife helps me so much, I can't find anything again.'

Simon laughed. 'I understand.'

'You've done a great job, Dad,' Lisa told him. 'It doesn't even smell like a garage.'

'Your mother's doing,' Richard said. 'She's been burning those candles of hers all afternoon. I'm surprised the fire department hasn't come by.' He grinned at his wife. 'They may be waiting until we light the cake.'

Rhonda playfully swatted her husband. 'Don't forget. Your birthday isn't far off, and you're older than I am.'

'Only by a year,' Richard protested.

'Those thirteen months make your cake brighter than mine,' she said. 'Now, go on. I know you're just dying to show Simon your toys.' She shooed him with her hands.

'Are you interested in cars, Simon?' Richard asked.

'I had a friend who restored a '57 Chevy when we were in college,' Simon replied. 'I watched more than I worked.'

'I can always use an assistant,' Richard declared. 'If I had another pair of hands it would only take me a minute to fix—'

'Don't you dare get oily,' Rhonda warned her husband. 'Simon? Make sure he doesn't.'

'Yes, ma'am,' both men said dutifully as they moved toward the tools and car parts strewn across a workbench. Lisa doubted if her father would heed her mother's warning.

'I wish your brothers would get here,' Rhonda fretted. 'They're in charge of barbecuing the hamburgers because I refuse to let your father near the fire. He starts talking and forgets what he's doing. I'd rather not serve lumps of coal.'

The door burst open and a blast of cold air accompanied Lisa's siblings and their families inside. Caught up in the task of organizing the food they'd brought, Lisa overheard her father introducing Simon to her elder brother, Andy, his wife, Mary, and eight-year-old son, Mark.

Next came Zane, her younger brother, and his date, Alison. Simon had already met her sister Jill, her husband, Kipp, and their two children.

While the women joined her around the food counter,

Lisa surreptitiously studied the men as they meandered to another corner. Both Zane and Andy took after their mother's side of the family. Although they resembled their grandfather in features and in stature, their eyes matched their father's perfectly.

And right now their attention bounced back and forth between her and Simon as broad grins crept across their faces. Andy waved hello from across the room, while Zane winked at her.

Heaven only knew what her father had told them, or what conclusions they'd drawn, but she intended to nip any romantic thoughts they might have before they had a chance to blossom.

Almost immediately the door opened again and the first of the guests began arriving. Andy and Zane began cooking the hamburger patties while Richard and Rhonda welcomed a growing number of people.

Lisa and the others replenished the pots of coffee and bottles of soda pop, along with whatever else ran low.

Kyle and Courtney were in their element, laughing and screaming with the other children. When the cooks announced dinner, Lisa happily took responsibility for Courtney's plate while Simon oversaw Kyle's. She drew a few stares and questioning glances as she sat down with Simon's small family, but she didn't care. She was having a wonderful time.

She should have known it wouldn't last.

Jill sat next to her. 'Don't look now,' she said in a tone that contradicted the smile on her face, 'but Bryan and his wife, Nancy, just came in.'

Lisa glanced in the direction of the door. Sure enough, her old flame, Bryan Lewis, and his pregnant wife, Nancy, had entered with Bryan's parents, Polly and Milton.

Rhonda gave her a helpless shrug from across the room, then graciously welcomed their neighbours.

'I see.' Her hand shook slightly as she cut Courtney's canned peaches into bite-sized pieces.

'Can you believe the nerve of that guy?' Jill snarled.

'Don't make a production out of this,' Lisa warned, trying to minimize the tense situation. Her brothers and sisters held more disdain for the man than she did. Other than a momentary shock, seeing Bryan didn't bother her. 'It's OK.'

Simon turned slightly to glance at the newcomers. 'So this is the infamous Bryan?'

'Afraid so.' In fact, as she studied his appearance, she wondered what she'd seen in him. He was shorter than Simon and possessed a wiry frame as opposed to Simon's more muscular one. Bryan's constant motion suddenly seemed irritating now that she'd spent time in Simon's calm presence. All in all, Bryan paled in comparison to the man beside her.

For the first time in a year, Lisa could honestly say that she wished Bryan and his wife all the best. And yet she knew everyone was waiting to see if she'd burst into tears like some slighted Victorian maiden.

'Oh, my gosh. Mom's bringing them over here. Has she lost her mind?' Jill nearly screeched.

'Would you just relax?' Lisa said, exchanging a glance with Simon and drawing peace from his presence. 'It isn't the end of the world, you know.'

Rhonda steered Polly, her son and his wife in their direction. 'Look who Polly brought to celebrate with us today. You remember Nancy?'

Lisa's smile was genuine. 'Yes. How are you?'

'Fine, thanks,' Nancy tentatively answered.

'I'd like you three to meet Lisa's boyfriend,' Rhonda

gushed. 'Simon Travers. He's one of the new doctors in Lisa's clinic.'

Lisa wanted to sink through the floor as she recognized her mother's attempt to show off her daughter's 'catch'. Apparently everyone else did, too, because a collective silence seemed to descend upon the room.

'I'm pleased to meet you,' Simon answered politely as the others murmured their own greetings.

'So, Bryan,' Lisa said in an attempt to make casual conversation, 'how's the hardware store?'

'Good.'

Nancy tucked her arm in his. 'He just got promoted to assistant manager.' She rubbed her swollen abdomen. 'It will certainly come in handy once we have an extra mouth to feed.'

'Congratulations,' Lisa said, meaning it.

'Speaking of food, there's plenty of it,' Rhonda broke in brightly, 'so help yourselves. Polly, you must try Lisa's salad.' Before they could say a word, she steered them away.

The moment had passed and the hum of conversation resumed. Much as she didn't like the idea of people imagining the importance of Simon in her life, Lisa was glad he'd come. If everyone considered his presence and her upcoming cruise, maybe they would finally stop linking her name with Bryan's and making the two synonymous with a broken engagement.

Although the rest of the evening was uneventful, Lisa was acutely conscious of being in the proverbial goldfish bowl. She mingled with the crowd, making a point of seeking out the Lewises from time to time. Although she inwardly apologized to Simon, she didn't let him stray too far from her side in order to encourage people to think of them as a couple.

To her surprise, Simon seemed to sense her plan. He became attentive and would either fling his arm around her shoulder if they were sitting, or around her waist if they were standing.

When her mother introduced Simon as 'Lisa's boyfriend' instead of 'Dr Travers' to total strangers, Lisa knew her scheme had been successful.

Too successful, in fact.

'What are you doing?' she muttered as Simon held a piece of her mother's birthday cake to her mouth.

'Playing my part,' he said. 'Have a bite.'

She complied, rather than risk having cake in her face. 'You don't have a part to play.'

He motioned in her mother's direction. 'Your mom doesn't seem to agree.'

'I'm so sorry,' Lisa moaned. 'I can explain.'

'We'll talk later,' he said, sliding a small piece onto a paper plate. 'This looks like Courtney's size, so I'll see if I can get her to stop playing long enough to taste it.'

Unable to argue without causing the scene she wanted to avoid, she simply glared at him.

He returned a smile. 'As one of my patients always told me, "Don't worry—everything works out in the wash."'

By eight-thirty, the children were turning cranky. Courtney had chocolate frosting smeared across her sleepy little face.

'We'll clean this tomorrow,' Rhonda decided. 'It's late. The kiddies need to be home in bed.'

'We can do it now,' Lisa said. 'It's not that late.'

'Don't argue, dear.' Her mother turned to Simon. 'Do you have plans for Thanksgiving?'

Simon's grin was sheepish. 'I haven't thought that far ahead.'

A this-would-never-do look appeared on Rhonda's face.

'Thanksgiving is only a few days away. You simply can't spend it by yourself. You must join us. I insist.'

Simon's unwavering gaze met Lisa's and a question appeared in the brown depths. 'I'm not sure... I don't want to impose.'

'It's not an imposition,' Rhonda declared. 'A few more mouths are always welcome.'

'I'll say,' Zane interrupted, 'otherwise we'll have to come back for turkey soup, turkey casserole and turkey surprise.'

'You may as well, Simon,' Lisa encouraged. 'I doubt if McDonald's will be open.'

'So little faith in my cooking abilities.'

Lisa cocked an eyebrow. 'You're cooking a turkey?'

'No, but I'm sure we won't go hungry—'

'I won't take no for an answer,' Rhonda declared. 'We'll expect you at noon.'

'All right,' he capitulated.

After a chorus of goodbyes, Lisa dressed Courtney in her winter coat while Simon helped Kyle. A short time later, they were in the car and on their way home.

'I'll help you put them to bed,' she offered as she pulled into Simon's driveway.

'Thanks.'

Lisa washed sleepy faces and tugged Courtney's night-gown over her head while Simon buttoned Kyle's pajamas. It seemed so domestic to kiss their foreheads and tiptoe from the room with Simon beside her.

She walked into the living room and stopped, conscious of Simon's nearby presence. It was time for her to leave, but she couldn't without clearing the air.

'I apologize for taking advantage of you,' she said. 'With Bryan there, I had to do something to ease the tension. Allowing my family to refer to you as my boyfriend seemed the best way to do it. I'm sorry if their comments embarrassed you.'

He stroked the side of her face with gentle fingertips. 'I wasn't embarrassed.'

Her breath caught in her throat. His light caress sent her blood pressure skyrocketing. 'I'll straighten them out tomorrow.'

'You don't have to on my account.'

'I don't?'

He bent his head as if to kiss her, but she drew back. 'If you're just being grateful about something…'

'Believe me, Lisa,' he said softly, 'at this moment, gratitude is the furthest thing from my mind.'

CHAPTER NINE

SIMON had wanted to indulge himself all evening and had waited patiently for his opportunity. This was it.

Logically, it wasn't wise to kiss Lisa until he'd explained his situation, but he couldn't wait. Tasting her mouth, having her in his arms with her body pressed against his, topped his list. The rest would come later.

If she rejected what he had to offer, then at least he would have this moment to remember.

'So now what?' she asked, sounding breathless as his lips trailed down her neck.

Yeah, Simon. Now what? His little voice spoke sarcastically and he knew he had to reveal all before things progressed both physically and emotionally.

He broke away and led her to the sofa. 'We probably should talk.'

Lisa's eyes slowly lost their hazy, passion-filled appearance. 'If we must.'

He smiled, thrilled by the plaintive note in her voice. 'I'm afraid so.'

'OK. What should we talk about?'

Simon sat beside her and loosely held her hand. 'I've been waiting for a woman like you.'

A slow smile spread across her face. 'Oh?' As he nodded, she asked, 'Then why did you let me believe otherwise?'

'Self-preservation, I suppose. Denying myself seemed the best say to handle the circumstances.'

'And now?'

'I don't want to deny myself any more,' he said simply. 'But you have a decision to make.'

'I don't want you to deny yourself either.'

Her eagerness pleased him. 'I appreciate your feelings, but you may change your mind after you hear what I have to say.' He might not like her choice, but he'd live with it.

She leaned back, her face expectant.

'I've already told you how Patsy and I depended on each other.'

At her nod, he continued, 'A long time ago, I dated a woman who hated it when I'd pay more attention to my sister than to her. At the time it seemed more important to establish Patsy's music career. Patsy became a stumbling block in our relationship and we eventually split up.

'Later, Patsy got married and started her own family, and I began to think about finding the right woman…' His voice died away.

'And now you've found her.'

He winced. 'Yes, but Patsy needs me again. I can't make any promises to you or consider my own future until she's through this rough spot. It could take a long time.'

'I see.'

'I'm all she has right now.'

'No, Simon,' she corrected. 'She has me and my entire family, too. I understand your desire to stand by your sister, but don't paint my family's picture with your family's colours. I'd never force you to choose between the two of us.'

In his heart he believed her sincerity, but his head had its doubts. 'As long as you understand my commitment to her and the children comes before all else…'

The excitement in Lisa's eyes dimmed. 'Let's wait and see what happens,' she said quietly. 'We'll take each day as it comes.'

*   *   *

On Saturday morning, Lisa stood on the porch of her parents' home, breathing in the crisp air as she watched Simon and the men in her family position the wrought-iron nativity set in the front yard. Zane had accused her of being more of a hindrance than a help and so she'd been relegated to supervise from the front porch.

The weekend was turning out better than she'd planned. Kyle and Courtney had fitted in so well with the rest of the Mallory children on Thanksgiving Day that by the time they went home they, too, were calling Richard and Rhonda 'Grandma' and 'Grandpa'.

Her brothers had treated Simon as if they'd known him for years. She had worried over Simon's reaction to their constant teasing, but he'd taken the good-natured heckling like a trouper. By Thursday afternoon, he'd got in the spirit of things and had delivered a few salvos of his own.

All in all, her family had accepted Simon and he had blended into their number perfectly.

It had been obvious that he'd fully expected her to say goodbye to him after he'd shared his feelings so honestly the other night. If she had, he wouldn't have tried to change her mind. He'd have allowed their mutual attraction to wither for lack of attention.

The notion was unthinkable.

Instead, she'd given herself an assignment to show him how her sense of duty matched his own. Patsy's high-profile life might not lend itself to confiding in or depending on a lot of people, but Lisa intended to prove to Simon that she wouldn't let him—or Patsy—down.

Once he learned these lessons, they could have a future. If he didn't…she'd worry about that when and if the time came.

'A little more to the left,' Lisa called out.

Andy, Zane, Kipp and Simon shared glances before they

put their shoulders to the silhouette of a wise man kneeling beside his camel. Most of Richard Mallory's home-made pieces were two-dimensional designs of appropriate holiday symbols and all were covered with strings of clear or multicolored blinking lights. Lisa was determined to place the kings *just so* around the manger scene.

'Too far. You've gone too far,' she yelled. 'Back to the right. Just a hair.'

Zane set his end down on the frost-covered ground. 'What do you mean, ''just a hair''? We have a half-acre of ground here. Who cares if this wise man isn't standing right next to the manger? I wouldn't want a mangy camel drooling over my baby's face anyway.'

Simon chuckled and she shot him an exasperated glare. 'Just a few inches,' she begged. 'Please.'

The four men glanced at each other and froze for an instant. As if they'd choreographed their motions, they each raised their ends, then immediately plopped them down on the ground.

'There's your few inches, sis,' Andy called out.

'You didn't move it at all,' she said accusingly.

'Hey,' Zane appeared affronted. 'An inch is an inch. Ask Simon.'

Simon laughed and raised his hands. 'You're not dragging me into the middle of this. I'm just another pair of hands.'

'It would still look better if you moved it over another inch or two,' Lisa groused. 'Don't you think so, Kipp?'

Lisa's brother-in-law, Kipp, resembled the two Mallory brothers in height, although he carried an extra twenty pounds on his frame and had a hairline which had started receding about the time he'd married her sister.

'Sorry. I refuse to incriminate myself.'

'Come on, guys,' she coaxed. 'The wise man and his camel are too far away from the crib.'

The men stepped back and studied the scene. 'Nope,' Zane said. 'Looks fine to me right where it is. It's too cold to stand out here and argue unless this is the only decoration you want us to set out, Madam Manager.'

Considering how a host of other seasonal items waited to be displayed, Lisa conceded. 'OK, but it wouldn't take so long if you'd put things exactly where I tell you.'

Andy nudged Simon. 'Holy Moses. Is she like this at work, too? How can you stand the nit-picking?'

Lisa quirked an eyebrow at Simon, waiting for his reply. His lips were red from the cold, as was the tip of his nose, and his eyes glistened with merriment. 'I'm seeing a whole new side to her.'

Zane shook his head. 'Unbelievable.'

The three tramped off to the garage and soon returned with several more pieces. Lisa idly watched them trudge with their loads to the driveway entrance. The men's banter drifted toward her on the crisp breeze and she couldn't tear her gaze off one man in particular.

Everything she'd ever wanted in a guy was all rolled up in the one neat package labeled Simon Travers. Her plan to show Simon another blueprint for a family had been a good one, but her objectivity had flown after the first day.

She'd fallen in love. Deeply, head over heels in love.

A flock of geese honked overhead and she shaded her eyes to study their V formation. Her spirits wanted to soar with her newfound knowledge, but how could they? He'd plainly stated that he wasn't interested in commitment right now.

If she failed this assignment, she was trapped. This time her heartache over Bryan wouldn't come close to what she'd feel if Simon willingly sacrificed their future for duty to his family.

Her fingers and toes reminded her of the cold. She stamped her feet to keep the blood circulating and dug her gloved hands into her pockets.

The door opened and Jill came out, wearing only her sweatshirt. 'Are they almost done?' she asked.

'Are you kidding?' Lisa said. 'At the rate they're working, we'll be finishing up with flashlights.' She watched as they each carried out another decoration while her father followed with heavy-duty extension cords slung around his shoulders.

The male voices drifted across the yard and the sound of a familiar chuckle brought a bitter-sweet smile to Lisa's face. She'd have recognized Simon's voice anywhere.

'He fits into the family well,' Jill commented.

Lisa nodded. 'I was surprised he agreed to help us get ready for our annual Mallory "yard lighting" ceremony, but he acts like he's having a good time.'

'So are the kids. Kyle and Courtney are having a ball with Tommy and Megan.' Jill rubbed her arms. 'Simon isn't anything like Bryan, is he?'

'Not at all.'

'He's the one you've been waiting for, isn't he?'

Lisa met Jill's gaze. 'Yes, but there are problems…'

Jill's teeth started to chatter. 'There always are,' she said. 'Good things don't come easy. You just can't give up. Hope springs eternal.'

Lisa groaned. 'Must you spout all your clichés?'

'Hey. This *is* the season of miracles.'

'I know.' But she was afraid to hope for one for herself.

'While you're pondering my sage advice, I'm going in where it's warm. The hot chocolate and coffee are ready whenever you are.'

'OK.' As Jill opened the door, Lisa stopped her. 'Thanks.'

Jill smiled and gave her a thumbs-up sign. Lisa turned back to watch the men work. Suddenly, she realized what they'd been doing while she'd been wool-gathering.

'Hey,' she called out, bounding down the steps toward them, 'those Christmas packages don't go there.'

Zane's groan was audible in spite of her being a fair distance away. 'Why not?'

'Because that's the spot for the candles,' she said.

'Why can't the presents be here this year?' he complained.

'Because they belong over by the Christmas tree,' she answered. 'Mom and I planned this for maximum effect, so don't make any changes.'

Andy grabbed his frame. 'I suppose these go on the other side of the yard.'

'As a matter of fact...'

Zane groaned again. 'Before we bring anything else out of storage, you'd better run through your diagram one more time.'

She dug a piece of paper out of her pocket. 'I thought you'd never ask.'

Zane nudged Andy. 'Why do we put up with this from her every year?'

'Because you love me,' she answered pertly. Her brothers might complain, but it was good-natured. 'As soon as you're all done, Jill has coffee and hot chocolate waiting.'

For the next thirty minutes Lisa strung the outdoor colored bulbs around a large evergreen which had become the backdrop Christmas tree to the three lighted packages. By the time she'd finished, the three men had added Santa, Rudolph, several angels and a snowman family to the yard, while her father had taken charge of supplying the electricity to each display.

'We saved the best for last,' she said as she propped the ladder against the house. 'The only thing missing is the sleigh.'

Andy groaned. 'Can't we skip the sleigh this year? It weighs a ton.'

'I know, but we have an extra body this year,' Lisa said, pointedly gazing at Simon as he returned her smile. Oh, what a fine extra body it was!

'Let's hurry up. I'm freezing.' With that, Andy led the way into the storage half of the garage. Lisa added her own muscles to the endeavor, and before long the five of them slowly made their way to the center of the yard with the unwieldy but authentic sleigh her father had found at an estate auction.

Andy stumbled and let out a curse as he dropped his end.

Lisa stared at her older brother. The sudden lines of pain on his face were too deep to be anything but real. 'Are you OK?'

He rubbed his lower back and nodded slowly. 'I tripped in one of those lousy ground squirrel holes. I'm fine.'

He picked up his section, then let it drop. 'Sorry, guys, but the sleigh either stays here or you're going to have to move it without me. I think something popped in my back.'

'I'm making an executive decision, sis,' Zane said. 'It's spending the holidays right here.'

No one argued. Lisa watched beads of sweat break out on her brother's forehead in spite of the cold temperature and wind chill. As they gathered around Andy, she glanced at Simon, hoping to see some reassurance in his eyes.

Simon had schooled his face into his familiar inscrutable doctor expression, but she knew him well enough to read his concern.

'Describe the pain for me,' he urged.

'It's like a knife in my lower back,' Andy said, rubbing at the spot.

'Does it go down one leg or both?'

Andy paused. 'Just down my left.'

'Can you walk?' Simon asked.

'Yeah.' Andy shuffled a step. 'I think so.'

With Zane and Simon on either side, they escorted Andy inside, helping him ascend the porch stairs.

Richard went ahead, opening doors and calling for his wife and Andy's wife, Mary. Both women came running, their faces white with worry. 'What's wrong?'

'Andy hurt his back.'

'Do you want to sit or lie down?' Mary asked her husband.

'The couch sounds pretty good right now.'

Lisa and Mary removed his coat as soon as he was standing by the sofa. Before Andy sank onto the cushions, Simon gently pulled his shirt out of his jeans.

'Where does it hurt?'

Andy pointed to an area in his lumbosacral region. Lisa knew that ninety per cent of disk problems occurred in this area of the spine.

'Have you had pain like this before?' Simon asked, as he carefully examined Andy's spinal column.

'No.'

'Any back injuries?'

'No.'

'If you can lie down, I'd like to do a few simple tests.'

Andy complied. Even with Lisa's and Simon's help, his face contorted with pain as he lowered himself onto the cushions. Simon placed one hand on Andy's hip-bone to stabilize the pelvis and the other under his ankle. He slowly raised the leg Andy had complained about. 'Does this hurt?'

'Yeah.'

'Where?'

'In my leg.'

'Not in your back?'

Andy hesitated before he shook his head. 'No. What's wrong?'

'A disk in your spine has either slipped or ruptured. Is there a history of joint degeneration in your family?'

Richard and Rhonda looked at each other while Simon glanced at Lisa. She shrugged while her parents denied any knowledge.

'I'd recommend an X-ray to rule out any other abnormalities,' Simon began, 'but tripping in that hole while you were carrying a heavy load probably twisted things out of place. Your family doctor will probably order an MRI and possibly a myelogram.'

'Andy hasn't been to a doctor in years,' Mary offered. 'Would you take him as a patient?'

'Sure. I'll work him in my schedule first thing on Monday. I'll have to clear it with my nurse, though.' He cast an amused glance in Lisa's direction. 'She runs a tight ship. I've even seen her whip out a stopwatch on occasion.'

'You wish,' Lisa retorted, grateful for Simon's effort to ease everyone's worry.

'What should we do until Monday?' Mary asked.

'Not a lot,' Simon answered apologetically. 'Bed rest, non-steroidal anti-inflammatory agents, heat application.'

'And after Monday?' Andy asked.

'More of the same. At least for the next week. Then we'll re-evaluate.'

Andy shook his head vehemently. 'I can't stay in bed for

a week. I have firewood to cut and customers waiting for delivery.'

'Sorry.' Simon was adamant. 'This is something that only time and rest will cure.'

'We have enough wood for the orders you were going to fill on Monday,' Mary told him.

'Yeah, but I don't have enough for next Saturday's deliveries.'

A furrow appeared on Mary's forehead. 'Your customers will have to wait, or call someone else if they're in a rush. You can't do it.'

'I have to, Mary,' he said. 'We need those orders.'

For a split second no one said a word, as if each family member pondered the implications of Andy's injury.

Lisa broke the silence first. 'I'll help. I'm the one who insisted we set out the sleigh. If you tell me about your customers, I can deliver their loads.'

'We're *all* helping,' Zane insisted. 'No arguments.'

Andy rubbed his face. 'I don't know. It's a lot to ask of you.'

'That's what families are for,' Rhonda told him. 'If we can't meet your orders, it won't be for lack of trying.'

Andy spoke to Simon. 'How long did you say I couldn't work?'

'Believe me, you won't *want* to work for at least a week. Maybe two. It just depends. Just remember, aggravating your condition can cause sensory and motor loss if the spinal-nerve compression isn't relieved. Let's see how you're doing by Monday. If you notice a progression in muscle weakness or numbness before then, call me right away.'

Andy sighed. 'All right.'

Mary grabbed his hand as she knelt on the floor next to the sofa. 'It'll be OK,' she murmured. 'We'll manage.'

'I guess we'll have to.' Andy cleared his throat. 'OK,

guys, you've just diversified into the firewood-cutting business.'

'We'll finish Dad's project before we start on yours,' Zane said. The men gulped down a cup of coffee before returning outside to connect the displays to electricity.

Before they had a chance to catch their collective breath, Zane insisted on cutting firewood while they still had daylight. Rhonda volunteered to watch the children and promised to have a pot of chili ready upon their return.

Lisa saw Simon's hesitation and guessed at its cause. 'You can go home,' she told him. Selfishly, she wanted him to stay, but he'd already put in a long day of physical labor. She couldn't ask for more.

Simon raised one eyebrow. 'Getting rid of me?'

Her face warmed as she realized how she must have sounded. 'You looked like you wanted to leave and didn't know how to slip away.'

'Actually, I was thinking about the kids. I hate to impose on your mother.'

Rhonda interrupted as she headed for the kitchen. 'It's not an imposition. They're playing so well together I hardly know they're around. Now, if you'll excuse me, I need to start our supper.'

Lisa touched his arm. 'Don't feel obligated to stick around. I'm sure you're tired and have other things you'd like to do…'

His mouth twitched with obvious amusement. 'Do I look like I need a nap?'

'No!' She was horrified. 'I just thought—'

Zane walked past and stuck his nose into their conversation. 'You'd better quit thinking, Sis, before you *really* offend Simon.' He continued on his way, whistling the 'Jingle Bell' chorus.

Simon smiled at her. 'I'm fine, chores and all. Even if I

wanted to leave, the kids would mutiny if I suggested it. Kyle and Courtney won't find me as entertaining a play-mate as someone their own age.'

'I don't want you to feel as if we're taking advantage of you.'

'I don't. Besides, I want to help.'

'You do?'

'Yeah.' He stuck his finger under her chin to close her mouth. 'If you don't hurry, they'll leave us behind.'

Zane, Jill and Kipp piled into Andy's truck for the drive to the shelter belt where Andy had permission to clear the dead trees and brush. Lisa and Simon rode with her father in his ancient jalopy.

The vehicle wasn't meant to impress anyone, however, it often did, simply because it still ran in its battered con-dition. The seat cushions were ripped, the inside passenger doorhandle was missing, the window lever was broken and the shock absorbers were nonexistent.

As they bounced down the rough track, Lisa struggled to keep her balance between the two men, but the jolts threw her against Simon's solid form. After the second time he wordlessly tucked her under his arm.

The ride smoothed out, thanks to her human anchor. Conscious of her father's smirk, she almost scrambled out of Simon's hold, before deciding to enjoy the moment while it lasted.

Simon asked, 'So your brother's having financial prob-lems?'

She forced herself to focus on the conversation and not on his body pressed against hers. 'They've been hit with everything from major repairs on both their vehicles to ter-mites.'

'Bummer.'

'Yeah. Andy started doing yard work this summer for

extra cash, and Mark helped. Once the weather turned cold, he switched to cutting firewood to supplement their income.'

Richard slowed to a crawl as they reached their destination. 'His mother and I wanted to give him some money to tide them over, but Andy wouldn't even take it as a loan. Too proud, I guess.'

Lisa stared through the windshield. 'I hope he'll recover quickly. I feel terrible about it. We should have moved the sleigh with the tractor.'

'It's not your fault,' Simon said. 'He could have tripped while he was carrying firewood and had the same thing happen. At least people were nearby at the time.'

'I guess so.'

Richard brought the truck to a halt. Because of Simon's missing handle, Zane opened the passenger door to let them out. 'Can you use a chain-saw, Simon?'

'It's been a while, but I'm sure I'll get the hang of it.'

'You've cut wood before?'

'Yeah. I've also trimmed trees, done yard work and painted houses. I tried being a plumber's assistant, but quit after a few days.'

'Why?'

'I hated crawling under houses. Too confining.'

Zane clapped him on the back. 'Don't mention your abilities too loudly, or Dad will make a list with your name on it.' He grinned. 'Isn't it great to be needed?'

As they began working, Lisa reflected on how timely Andy's injury had been. This was a perfect opportunity to show Simon how her family stuck together.

By Monday morning Andy had shown some improvement, but Simon insisted on a regular X-ray and an MRI. 'So we have an idea of what we're dealing with,' he said. 'Depending on what we find, chiropractic treatments may help.'

So, while Mary left with her protesting husband, Lisa called the hospital radiology department to schedule the appointment. Just as she hung up the phone, Alice poked her head into the small lab.

'It's the first of December,' she said without preamble. 'Have you found a gift for Dr Travers yet?'

Lisa winced. 'No, but I'm working on it.'

'I certainly hope so. Our party is on the nineteenth. You have exactly three weeks to come up with something spectacular.'

Spectacular, she thought glumly. Although she'd found out more details about Simon's life, none of the information was helpful in determining what he'd want *now*, or what would be appropriate as a gift. He might have trimmed trees, mowed yards and painted houses in his lifetime, but that didn't mean he wanted a chain-saw, a lawnmower or painting supplies.

With everything that had happened at her parents' home this past weekend, no one had even had time to think about Christmas, let alone discuss it.

As for Simon's gift, she could only hope for a flash of insight when they took Kyle and Courtney to the mall this week to visit Santa's Workshop.

In the meantime, she had a roomful of patients waiting to see Simon, starting with Fanny Grant, a seventy-year-old Alzheimer's patient.

'How did you hurt your arm?' Lisa asked Fanny as Simon began sewing up the two-inch gash above her wrist.

Fanny stared at her arm and shook her head in obvious puzzlement before she glanced at her daughter, Louise. 'Did I run into a door?'

Louise drew an audible breath. 'No, Mother. You fell,

remember? She also has a knot on her shin but, as far as I can tell, she's OK otherwise.'

Fanny glanced around the room. 'Where's the television? Why is the TV missing?'

'We're at the doctor's office, Mom,' Louise patiently explained.

'I'm not sick. Are you sick?' Fanny asked.

'No, Mom. The doctor is fixing your arm.'

'Oh. That's right.' Fanny eyed Lisa suspiciously. 'Who are you?'

'I'm Dr Travers's nurse.'

'I used to sew,' Fanny remarked as Simon slid the needle through her anesthetized skin. 'My eyesight's not too good so I quit.'

'I'll bet you were a wonderful seamstress,' Lisa said, admiring Simon's neat row of black stitches.

'All done,' he said as he tied off the last knot. 'Keep it clean and dry.'

'I'll try,' Louise said, 'but Mother doesn't always cooperate.'

'I understand,' Simon said. He looked right at Fanny. 'Don't get your arm wet or dirty. Can you do that?'

Fanny's frail frame stiffened. 'Of course, young man. I've been taking care of myself since long before you were even a glimmer in your mother's eye.'

Simon smiled. 'OK. Don't forget.' He addressed Louise. 'Is she having any other problems we should know about?'

'No. If she didn't have Alzheimer's, she'd be in marvelous shape. She'll probably outlive me.'

Fanny held out her arm, her face a picture of bewilderment. 'What's this for?'

Frustration appeared on Louise's face. 'See what I mean?'

Simon closed Fanny's medical chart. 'Have you been

able to take a break? You know, get away from the responsibility for a while?'

'I wish,' she said fervently. 'The kids are coming home from college for Christmas and I want this to be a special time for them, but Mom isn't making it easy. I can't even decorate the house because she carries everything off. I don't dare set out any packages for fear they'll never be seen again.'

Fanny tugged on Lisa's sleeve. 'Who are you?'

'I'm the doctor's nurse.'

Fanny sat down in her chair again, looking like a frail bird on a perch.

'I really can't complain. Mom's not violent or belligerent. Other than constantly misplacing things, she's harmless. It's becoming tiresome, though, because I waste so much time looking for whatever's missing. I spent an hour last night searching for a can opener. I tried locking the cabinets, but somehow she manages to open them.'

'Have you considered hiring someone to take over for a day or two to relieve you?'

Louise snorted. 'I'd love a break. In fact, the thought of a vacation with maid service is pure heaven. I can't find anyone who would watch her for more than a few hours at a time.'

'You're not much use to your mother if you wear yourself out.'

'I know, but what can I do?'

'The nursing home offers overnight stays for people like your mom,' Simon said. 'They'll also take them on a daily basis if the caretakers need a few hours of free time for errands or appointments.'

Louise's demeanor seemed to perk up. 'I hadn't heard of such a thing.'

'It's a relatively new program,' he went on. 'We have a

brochure somewhere, but why don't you give them a call? The girls can explain it in more detail.'

Fanny stood up and stared at Lisa as if Lisa had sprouted horns. 'You're a call girl? I've never met one before.'

It took Lisa a moment to follow the convoluted train of Fanny's logic. By the time she had, she saw the laughter in Simon's eyes.

Louise's face turned pink. 'We were talking about *calling* a *girl*, Mom. On the telephone. This has nothing to do with Dr Travers's nurse.' She glanced at Lisa and shrugged.

Fanny's eyes grew wide. 'You're calling one of those phone sex numbers? I watch TV. I know all about them. Call 1-800—'

Lisa started to laugh while Louise tried to correct her mother's thinking. 'No, Mother. We're not discussing phone sex. Put that thought right out of your head this instant!'

Fanny leaned closer to Simon. 'They think I just fell off the turnip truck yesterday, but I didn't. I know about these things. Barbara Walters did a special on it last night.'

'You didn't watch television last night, Mother.'

Fanny waved her hand. 'Doesn't matter. I still saw it on TV. So it must be true.'

'Let's go, Mom.' Louise hurried her mother from the room while Lisa found the brochure in question. As soon as the two women left, Simon cornered Lisa in the lab.

'First a call girl and then phone sex. To think I'd pegged you as the shy, retiring type.'

She smiled. 'Yeah. I'm just full of surprises. You know what they say, "still waters run deep." By the way, when's the last time *you* had a vacation?' After filling in the gap for his family, perhaps he needed some R and R time of his own. The clinic's gift budget could cover a week-end away.

He shrugged. 'I don't know. A couple of years, I guess.'

'Is there someplace you'd like to go?'

A slow smile crossed his face. 'Are you offering to take me?'

The memory of Lorna Rajewski's honeymoon suite suggestion popped into her mind. Lisa's face burst into flame, or so it felt. 'Well, no, I just wondered…with Christmas and all…' Geez, she was babbling. 'I'm making conversation, so give me a break.'

'There are a few places I wouldn't mind visiting, but taking a vacation by myself isn't my idea of a fun time.'

If they gave him a weekend trip to St Louis, they couldn't expect him to go alone. Because she didn't like the idea of someone else accompanying him, she immediately scratched the idea off her list.

'Why do you want to know?'

'Just curious,' she said nonchalantly. She had three weeks to find the perfect, *spectacular* gift, three weeks to teach Simon the real truth about family ties before she left on the cruise she didn't want to take right now. Three weeks to show how those bonds should be strong enough to love through thick and thin, yet loose enough so as not to stifle.

The pressure of her Christmas assignment was starting to bear down. Time was running out.

CHAPTER TEN

ON FRIDAY night, Courtney tugged on Lisa's hand impatiently and her voice rose an octave in her excitement. 'Are we really gonna see Santa?'

The child's enthusiasm was contagious. 'We won't leave until we do,' Lisa promised. 'Right, Simon?'

'Absolutely. Do you remember what you're going to tell Santa?'

Courtney nodded. 'A doll and a kitchen set and a video game and puzzles and a new dress and a car and...' She screwed her face into a frown, as if trying to recall the rest of her list. 'And for Mommy to take us home.'

'Sounds like a tall order for Santa to fill,' Simon said, steering their group through the hordes of other adults on the same mission. 'Do you think you'll get everything you've asked for?'

'I been good this year,' Courtney said sincerely. 'But if he doesn't have 'nuff time to make the toys, then I just want him to make Mommy better.'

The child's faith touched Lisa's heart. 'I'm sure he will do his very best to give you everything you want,' she said. 'Now, Kyle? What do *you* want for Christmas?'

Kyle's brown eyes sparkled and he started to skip alongside them. 'A train set, Lego, a Nebraska Cornhuskers football uniform, the new PlayStation video-game system, some movies and a new coat.' Then, as an afterthought, he added, 'I've been good this year, too.'

Simon leaned close to Lisa's ear. 'Did you get all that? We don't want to forget anything they mentioned.'

'Not to worry,' Lisa told him, her voice loud enough for Simon to hear her over the crowd and yet low enough so the children couldn't. 'I printed their lists for Santa and made a copy for us. They're right here.' She patted her shoulder-bag.

'What a lifesaver,' he said fervently. 'What would I do without you?'

'I guess you'd better keep me,' she quipped lightly. 'Goodness! Will you look at that line of people?'

'Let's find the end before it gets any longer.' Simon manoeuvred his way through the crowd, holding onto Courtney's and Lisa's hands while Lisa hung onto Kyle.

To their surprise, the queue moved fairly quickly. Each step forward added to the children's already high level of anticipation. Too excited to stand still, they dashed around the benches where tired shoppers rested their weary bones.

Simon nudged Lisa. 'After everything we've done this week, I'd assumed they wouldn't have any more energy.'

'I know what you mean. Between decorating your tree on Monday, driving around town on Tuesday to look at the lights, visiting the living nativity scene at the church Wednesday evening, baking cookies last night and shopping tonight, we haven't had a free moment. Come to think of it, you haven't had a chance to swim.'

'Maybe next week,' he said.

'Our schedule shouldn't be as hectic,' she said thoughtfully. 'As for tomorrow, I'm looking forward to sleeping late.'

'I can't,' he mourned.

'Why not?'

'They both wake up at the crack of dawn to watch cartoons. I'll be lucky to sleep past seven.'

Lisa laughed. 'You poor thing.'

'Hey,' he protested. 'You'd better show the proper

amount of sympathy or I'll give them permission to spend the night at *your* house.'

'You poor, poor thing.' This time she added the properly commiserating note to her tone.

He grinned. 'That's better.'

Courtney dashed past with Kyle on her heels. 'Slow down,' Lisa admonished as they started to circle her and Simon. 'You're going to slip and fall or run into someone.'

'We'll be careful,' Kyle said.

'From the way Kyle's running around, I can't believe Jill said he's acted sick at times,' Simon said as they watched the two grab hands to gaze at the fountain's red and green underwater lights.

Lisa studied the little boy. 'I've noticed it, too. He'll act normal, then he'll seem too quiet.'

'Are we talking about the same boy you just scolded for running?'

'You know what I mean. Call it mo—' She'd been about to say 'mother's' but caught herself in time. 'Intuition, but he's not up to par.'

'After-effects from the holiday rush,' Simon said. 'Not to mention the sugar. Those two have practically eaten every one of those cookies your mom sent home with us.'

'Confession time,' she teased. 'You ate your fair share if my spies are to be believed.'

'I had to make sure they were edible,' he protested. 'It was a dirty job, but someone had to do it.'

She smiled. 'Yeah, right.'

Kyle and Courtney came barreling toward them. Before Lisa could caution Kyle to slow down, Kyle bumped into her and she teetered. Simon immediately grabbed her.

He pressed his mouth against her ear. 'Are you all right? Nothing damaged, I hope.'

'No,' she choked out, enjoying the brief contact and wishing she could manage to make it last.

A woman with long dark hair dressed in an elf costume approached them. 'Would you like your children to have their picture taken with Santa?'

Lisa regained her footing and stared at Simon, her composure slightly ruffled by the reference to 'your children' because it reminded her of her wishful fantasies. He, however, didn't bat an eyelash.

'Yes, we would,' he said smoothly. 'OK, kids. After pictures, then it'll be your turn to talk to Santa.'

Awe appeared on Courtney's face as she took the elf's hand and walked down the lane to Santa's house. Kyle slowed and followed at a sedate pace, although he had a distinct bounce in his step and a grin stretched from ear to ear.

Lisa stood near the candy-cane fence, conscious of Simon's shoulder rubbing hers and his hand on her waist.

'I never thought I'd say this, but I'm enjoying this Christmas more than I thought I would,' she admitted as she watched the woman snap the children's photos before helping them climb on Santa's lap.

'Me, too.'

'In fact—'

At that moment, someone came from behind and grabbed her elbow. 'Lisa Mallory? Long time no see! How the heck are you?'

Simon dropped his arm and his blood pressure spiraled upward at the sight of Lisa in a blond giant's bear hug. Everything about this man set his teeth on edge, from his fancy business suit and polished wingtips to the ruby ring on his finger.

'Jason Miner!' she said, her smile in the megawatt range. 'I haven't seen you for ages.'

'Just moved back to town,' he said. 'If I'd known you were still here, I'd have retired sooner!'

Lisa laughed. 'Jason, there's someone I'd like you to meet. Jason, Simon Travers. Jason played professional football until he was sidelined with a knee injury.'

Simon shook his hand, wishing the man would move along. Mr Pro-ball was encroaching on *his* time with Lisa.

'Hey, I saw Savanna and she told me about your cruise,' Jason said. 'Sounds like a good idea. I may have to go along to keep you girls company.'

'Now, Jason,' Lisa chided, although Simon didn't miss the sparkle in her eyes, 'we'd never see you because you'd be hustling all the other available women.'

'Not a chance, sweet cakes.' He flashed a fourteen-carat grin. 'I've got to make up for lost time with you.'

Simon suddenly realized that Lisa could meet some other fellow on this cruise, someone who would fall in love with her and promise those things he wasn't ready to promise.

Next year at this time she could be shopping for Christmas presents and standing in line for a visit with Santa with another man at her side.

The prospect was sobering.

'Heard you finally got rid of Bryan,' Jason continued. 'I never thought he was the right guy for you.'

Lisa shook her head, her humor obvious. 'I suppose you think you are?'

Jason leaned closer to Simon. 'I was the first kid brave enough to steal a kiss from Lisa when we were in the second grade.'

'Really?' Simon almost mentioned a case in the news where a child who'd done the same thing had been charged with sexual harassment, but he held his tongue.

'Don't forget to tell how you got a bloody nose for your efforts,' Lisa teased.

Simon smiled at the picture.

Jason dismissed her remark. 'Yeah, well, I don't get bloody noses now.'

Wait long enough and see, Simon thought darkly.

'Unca Simon, Lisa, Lisa. Lookee what we got from Santa!' Courtney came up at a run, holding her candy cane aloft. Kyle followed closely behind.

'I tolded Santa what I wanted and he said he'd see what he could do,' Courtney chirped. 'I can't wait!'

'What did Santa tell you, Kyle?' Simon asked.

'He said his elves liked to make trains. Can we go now?'

Saved by a child. 'Of course.' Simon turned to Jason. 'Nice meeting you.'

'Same here.' Jason leaned over and kissed Lisa's cheek. 'I'll call you some time.'

Two red spots appeared on her cheeks. 'Sure. I'm in the book.'

Jason had hardly taken three steps when Courtney tugged on Lisa's coat. 'Why did that man kiss you?'

Simon noticed how Lisa avoided his gaze. 'Because we're friends.'

Courtney stared up at Simon. 'Are you and Lisa friends?'

'Yes, Court. We are.'

'Then how come you don't kiss her?'

'Because…' It's hard to stop with just a kiss. He couldn't think of a reply suitable for small ears.

'Because your uncle is shy and doesn't like to kiss anyone in front of other people,' Lisa supplied.

'He kisses *me* in front of other people,' the little girl added.

'That's different,' Simon tried to explain.

'Why?'

''Cos you're a kid and Lisa's a grown-up,' Kyle said crossly. 'Don't be such a dork.'

Courtney stamped her foot. 'I'm not a dork.'

'Are, too.'

'Am not.'

Simon interrupted the argument and motioned to the window of a nearby toy store. 'Is this the train you want, Kyle?'

Kyle's face brightened. 'It is! Can we go inside and look?'

Simon checked his watch. 'For a few minutes. We need to find a gift for your mom.'

After fifteen minutes of oohing and aahing over the latest and greatest toys, Simon herded them out of the store and toward the next.

'What was this about bossy nurses and stopwatches?' she joked as he hastened them into the craft store with the angel tree in the window.

'Just trying to keep us on task. Shopping isn't one of my favourite pastimes.'

'And what *is* a favourite pastime?'

'Swimming. Watching a good movie.' He spied a yellow glass canary. 'Hey, kids. Doesn't your Mom collect birds?'

Courtney and Kyle pressed their noses to the display case. 'Yup,' Kyle announced. 'That yellow bird would be pretty.'

'Mommy has a yellow bird,' Courtney argued. 'A blue bird would be nicer.'

Kyle squared his small jaw in obvious stubbornness. Tempers would flare unless Simon intervened. 'Why don't we buy them both?' he suggested. 'She'll love to have one from each of you.'

Appeased by his solution, both children watched as the clerk carefully packed the glass canary and bluebird in separate boxes and gift-wrapped each one.

'Can we go home now?' Kyle whined as they sauntered from the store. 'I'm tired.'

'Leaving has my vote,' Lisa said. After the day's hectic pace at work, and fighting the mall crowd, she was more than ready for peace and quiet.

'Then home it is.'

In what had become a well-honed routine, Lisa stayed at Simon's until baths had ended and bedtime stories had been read.

Ordinarily, she left immediately after saying her good-nights because she had odd jobs to do at home. Tonight, however, she intended to break her habit and say yes when Simon asked her to stay. Time was marching on and she still didn't have the foggiest notion of an appropriate gift for him. For all she was around Simon almost constantly, she was failing miserably in the idea department.

With ideas in mind, Courtney had floored her with her talk of Simon kissing her. Ever since the little girl had mentioned it, Lisa hadn't been able to take her mind off the kisses they'd shared. Having two half-pints underfoot, it made it difficult to encourage a romantic interest.

At least Jason's hug had proved an immutable fact. She didn't want anyone else's arms around her, except Simon's. Perhaps it was time to remind him of how fulfilling his duty to Patsy wouldn't fulfill his own personal needs.

While she waited for him to reappear, she idly examined the bookcase in the corner. Fiction, ranging from westerns to adventure and mystery, filled the top two shelves. *Moby Dick*, *Treasure Island* and *20,000 Leagues Under the Sea* were only a few of the classic tales standing on the third shelf, along with a variety of American history books.

What startled her most were the volumes of reference books on navigation. She also found pictorial volumes on every seaworthy vessel imaginable, both present-day and historical. She doubted if the public library owned such an extensive collection.

'If you ever suffer from insomnia, I have the perfect reading material for you,' he quipped as he came into the room, clutching two glasses of wine.

She accepted one, realizing that he had also changed tactics. Instead of offering her a nightcap, he'd simply made her one, as if knowing she wouldn't refuse.

Raising the rosé to her lips and taking a sip, she said, 'This is delicious.'

'It came highly recommended.'

'You must have been sure I'd stay.'

'I'd hoped,' he corrected her.

Lisa's insides quivered as she wondered how far ahead he'd planned this strategy. Forcing herself to remain calm, she motioned to the bookcase. 'Tell me how someone who lives a land-locked life is in love with the ocean.'

He sipped his wine before he spoke. 'Sea-faring stories fascinated me. I could imagine a man standing on the bridge of his ship and staring at an endless horizon. The wind rustling through his hair. An entire sky filled with stars. Fighting against the elements in order to achieve his dream.'

'Maybe you have a pirate hidden in your family tree.'

'I don't think so. But just think of how fortunate those men were. At a time when it took days to go the shortest distances, they travelled all over the world.'

'And had a girl in every port.'

He burst out laughing. 'All part of the fantasy. Should I ask what your fantasy is?'

'Do you really want to know?'

His gaze didn't waver from hers. 'Yes.'

It was now or never. She placed her wineglass on the

coffee-table, then wrapped her arms around his neck. 'This.'

She pressed her mouth to his and he responded to her invitation. An instant later she was plastered against him, surrounded by his loving embrace.

This was her fantasy—or at least the start of it.

She poured every ounce of feeling she possessed into that kiss, allowing every hope, every dream, every desire for their future to make itself evident.

Everything about him seemed to become a part of her. His breath, his scent, and his taste combined with hers to the point where she could no longer differentiate between what was his and what was hers.

She wanted this moment to last for a lifetime, wishing for a way to capture it in more than a memory.

Slowly, his lips travelled a path along her cheekbones, her forehead and her eyes, seeming to ignite a trail of unquenchable flames.

'We shouldn't be doing this,' he muttered.

'Probably not,' she agreed. Yet she was willing to do whatever it took to show him what he would receive if he allowed himself this gift and what he would give up if he chose to shut her out of his life.

'Unca Simon?'

Courtney's small voice cooled Lisa's ardour as quickly as a bucket of ice water. She stepped away from Simon, feeling oddly bereft by the sudden loss of contact.

'What did you need, Court?' Simon asked.

'Is tomorrow the day we're gonna see Mommy?'

'No, hon. We're going on Sunday.'

'OK.' She rubbed her eyes. 'G'night.'

Lisa froze. 'You'll see Patsy on Sunday?'

'Yeah. Her therapist thought it would be a good idea if she saw the kids.'

Lisa counted to five and tried to hide the hurt she felt over being kept in the dark over such an important aspect of his life. 'When were you going to tell me?'

'The kids and I talked about it earlier in the week, but—'

'You knew earlier in the week that you were travelling to Branson?' The hurt intensified.

'Our plans weren't definite,' he said defensively. 'Besides, you're contending with your own family problems. You don't need to worry about mine.'

'This isn't a question of worrying, it's a question of courtesy. Whether you went or not, Simon, you should have at least mentioned the possibility to me.'

'You couldn't have come along, anyway. You're cutting wood this weekend for Andy, remember?'

'That's not the point,' she ground out, irritated by his practical thinking. 'Friends keep each other informed of what's important in their lives.'

'You're making more of this than it is,' he began.

'I don't think so.' A horrible thought came to her. 'This is an issue of trust, isn't it? You didn't tell me because you didn't trust me to support your decision.'

'No.' His answer seemed half-hearted.

'It's true, isn't it? You honestly thought I'd try and talk you out of going.'

She started to pace. 'To think that after all the time we've spent together, after everything you've seen my family do, you still expect me to pull you away from Patsy.'

'No,' he repeated, shaking his head.

She blinked away the moisture forming in her eyes. 'I've been such a fool to think you'd see me for what I am.'

'I do.'

Lisa trembled with suppressed fury. 'No, you don't. You carry this picture of someone else, not me.' She yanked her coat out of the closet. 'I'm sorry you feel as if you're the only one who can ever give Patsy moral support. I'm sorry you believe me so shallow and insecure that I'd keep you from her.'

'You're wrong.'

'Am I? I doubt it.' Now that she'd started, she couldn't stop.

'It's amazing how you can see Fanny's daughter, Louise, drag herself down, trying to assume total care of her mother, yet you can't see how you're putting yourself in the same position. Have you ever considered who Patsy will rely on if something should happen to *you*?'

She drew a deep, calming breath. 'I had actually considered giving up my cruise to stay in town for the holidays... I must have been crazy. The thing I'm most sorry for, though, is for falling in love with you.'

Lisa didn't wait to see Simon's reaction to her speech. She turned and literally ran to her car, eager to be alone before her tears of disappointment fell.

The phone rang, but she didn't answer it. Instead, she nursed her heartache through her music for hours on end until she finally vowed to let Simon have the lonely life he wanted.

Perhaps she'd overreacted, but this small incident had hammered home a truth she hadn't wanted to face. If he couldn't trust her with something so small, then he'd never trust her in something more important.

Few people knew of her love for him, so at least she'd be spared a repeat of those days following the break-up of her engagement. A blessing, indeed.

As for her promise to Patsy, she'd done all the Christmassy things with the children this week. If Kyle and Courtney wanted to see her, Simon could drop them off at her house. It would be hard enough to see him at work—she didn't want to extend her agony into the evening hours.

The next morning, thanks to her foresight in preparing a detailed gift list, she purchased each remaining item in record time and without any emotion. She refused to think about Simon's gift at all.

As she carried her last package to her car, something bright and shiny in the window of an import shop caught her eye. She stopped and saw the sun reflecting off the most beautiful hand-blown glass figures. On a soft bed of velvet in the center of the display stood the most detailed glass clipper ship in a bottle, and it almost seemed to have Simon's name on it.

She went inside for a closer look. It was exquisite, expensive and, to use Alice's words, *spectacular*. It was perfect.

'May I help you?' the elderly gentleman behind the counter asked.

'I'd like the ship.'

'A wonderful choice. For someone special, no doubt.'

'My boss,' she said shortly, unwilling to admit to anything else.

'He'll love this. Especially after he learns it was hand-blown in Spain. The certificate of authenticity is in the box.'

'Thank you.' She wrote a check to cover the amount, then tucked the receipt in her purse.

Yes, Simon would love his gift. No doubt he'd imagine himself at the helm, sailing off on a quest for adventure. An adventure where he trusted only a handful of people, where a wife wasn't welcome because she might tear him away from his obligations rather than help him meet them.

She sighed as she slid into her car. Her Christmas assignment was now officially completed, but the knowledge didn't give her the satisfaction she'd expected.

She'd hoped to break the cycle of depressing Christmases this year and, instead, had only cemented her dislike in place. Basking in the sun sounded like the perfect escape from a season that would never mean the same again.

Simon's weekend ticked by slowly without Lisa to brighten the hours. After seeing her every day, her nightly phone call wasn't the same. He felt her absence keenly, as did the children. Even though the same snow that postponed their trip made the area a winter wonderland, the holiday season had lost its luster.

He couldn't stop his mind from replaying the final scene with Lisa. Hindsight being twenty-twenty, he should have trusted her with his plans. From the moment Lisa had asked about his trip, he knew he'd made a monumental mistake. Lisa wouldn't have talked him out of going—he knew that now—but part of him had refused to take the chance. If she *had* tried to dissuade him, he didn't know how he could have dealt with his shattered image of the woman he loved.

He loved Lisa. Unfortunately, he'd crushed her spirit, as well as her trust, and he didn't know how to repair the damage. An apology wasn't enough. Trust, while easily broken, wasn't easily mended. Neither had he realized the inner pain he'd caused her until he'd felt the sting of rejection for himself. He'd once thought he could live with her decision to walk away—he'd been wrong.

He *was* also like Fanny Grant's daughter, Louise—shouldering the full responsibility when there were other people, other avenues, available. Especially people like Lisa, who seemed to have a heart large enough for everyone. Maybe in time she'd find it in herself to forgive him.

Monday finally arrived and Simon went to work with

both eagerness and trepidation. Lisa's chilly reception didn't come as a surprise, although he'd expected Andy to rake him over the coals during his follow-up visit. Her brother hadn't said a word, which meant she hadn't confided in her family. Instead, Andy had gleefully accepted the news that he could resume light duties.

Simon watched her closely all day, hoping to see a sign of a softening attitude, but found none. She politely assisted him when necessary, and acted as professionally as ever, but her attitude toward him could have frozen water.

Tuesday and Wednesday passed in the same manner. His attempts at casual conversation failed until he reluctantly admitted defeat. There had to be some way to reach her, but he didn't know how.

As he lay in bed that night, contemplating his next move, Kyle trudged into his bedroom. His lower lip quivered as he rubbed his abdomen. 'Unca Simon? I don't feel good.'

Simon sat up. 'What's wrong?'

'My tummy hurts. Here.'

'Too many cookies again today?' Simon teased.

Kyle started to cry. 'I didn't have any. It hurts. I want Mommy. Or Lisa. She can make it feel better. Why won't she visit any more? I miss her terrible bad.'

He felt Kyle's forehead and found him warm to the touch. The next second, Kyle began retching. Instantly Simon carried him to the bathroom.

During the next hour, his gut told him this was more than a simple stomachache or the flu. Immediately he went for the phone and punched in Lisa's number.

At the sound of her sleep-filled voice, he said, 'Please, don't hang up. I'm taking Kyle to the hospital and I need you.'

'What's wrong?' Concern had replaced the diffident tone he'd heard over the past few days.

'I'm not sure.'

CHAPTER ELEVEN

LISA didn't hesitate. 'I'll be right there.' She dressed in record time and drove through town as fast as she dared.

She rushed into the house without knocking and heard the unmistakable sounds of Kyle retching. She went into the bathroom.

'How is he?' she asked, taking in the view of the little boy clutching the toilet and Simon—goodness, but he was a sight for sore eyes even at this hour—hovering over him like a guardian angel.

'Temp's up. Lower quadrant pain. Seems to be more on the right, but he's a little vague about its exact location. I'm taking him in for lab work. Hopefully a CBC will give us more clues.'

Lisa bundled Kyle warmly in his coat and wrapped him in a blanket. 'Take my car,' she said, handing Simon a bowl in case Kyle needed it during their short trip. 'It's already warm.'

Simon hefted the little boy in his arms. 'We're on our way.'

Lisa kissed Kyle's cheek. 'See you soon.'

Kyle closed his eyes and laid his head on Simon's shoulder.

Although she knew it would take time to make the diagnosis, she waited impatiently for news. At three a.m. the phone finally rang.

Simon sounded tired. 'His CBC and ultrasound were inconclusive. Benington thinks it's his appendix, but he wants to wait and see what his white count does. We'll do another test at seven. I'm going to hang around until then.'

'OK. If you need anything, you'll call?'

Lisa didn't hear any hesitation on the other end. 'Yes,' he said. 'I will.'

At seven Lisa woke Courtney, and after a quick trip through a McDonald's drive-thru for breakfast she went to Jill's house and explained the situation. After that, she dashed home to shower and change, before going to the hospital.

She met Simon outside Kyle's room, talking into his cellphone. His frustration was obvious from the way he ran his free hand through his hair. A dark shadow covered his chin and his clothes appeared somewhat wrinkled. A second later, he snapped the cover closed and muttered a curse.

'How is he?' she asked.

'They're taking him to surgery as soon as they get an OR free. His white count jumped to over fifteen thousand.'

'Does Patsy know?'

'She's leaving Branson right now on a corporate plane, but the closest I can get her to Farmington is a private airstrip about thirty miles away. I've got to pick her up.' He glanced around. 'Where's Courtney?'

'At Jill's. Why don't you stay here while I arrange to meet your sister?'

He frowned. 'I don't know…'

'Don't argue, Simon. You should be here to oversee Kyle's surgery. Zane will be happy to play chauffeur.'

'Are you sure?'

She gave him a disgusted glare and held out her hand. 'Phone, please.' After he'd placed it in her palm, she shooed him into Kyle's room. 'Go do your doctor thing while I do mine.'

As soon as she'd given Zane his instructions and sworn

him to secrecy about his passenger's identity, she called the clinic and asked SueEllen to cancel Simon's appointments. After informing everyone who needed to know about the situation, she waited in Kyle's room with Simon and did her best to reassure the little boy.

Patsy arrived shortly before nine. She only had time to give a sleepy Kyle a quick hug and a kiss before the surgical staff had wheeled him away.

Zane pulled Lisa aside. 'Good thing you warned me ahead of time about Patsy Carter. The media must have had wind of her arrival because I had to fight them off in droves to get to her. They're all in the hospital lobby, clamouring for an interview. A regular pack of vultures,' he finished in a disgusted tone.

'Thanks for doing the favor,' she said.

'How about a cup of coffee?'

'No, thanks.' With Patsy here, she was extraneous. 'My job is finished. It's time to go.'

'Other than this excitement with Kyle, how have things been going?' Patsy asked after they'd been told Kyle was in Recovery and doing well.

'Fine.' Simon filled two disposable cups from the coffee-pot provided in the surgical waiting room and passed one to her before he sank into an overstuffed chair.

'You don't look so fine. And don't tell me it's because you stayed up all night with my son. Something's on your mind. Or should I say some*one*?'

Simon didn't know where to begin, but his sister had opened this Pandora's box, so he decided to air the contents.

'You know I'd do anything to help you and the kids.'

'Yes.' She drew out the word.

'Have I been too overbearing? Too controlling? Have I enabled you to become too dependent on me?'

Patsy smiled. 'Have you been talking to my therapist? We've been discussing this same subject.'

'No kidding?'

'You're an extremely decisive person,' she began slowly. 'You always have been. It was easier to lean on you than to develop my own backbone.'

'It took backbone to succeed in the music industry,' he reminded her.

She smiled. 'Yes, but you were waiting in the wings to pick me up if I fell. When we were younger it was always us against them because we didn't have anyone else to rely on. Now things are different. Things *have* to be different.'

'It sounds as if you've covered a lot of ground with your therapist in a short amount of time.'

She rose and hugged him. 'I have. I know I can always count on you, but I have to start handling things myself. I can't call you to fix every little thing that goes wrong in my life. It's not fair to either of us.' She paused. 'Or to Lisa.'

He jerked his head around to meet her gaze. 'What—?'

She smiled. 'I don't know her well, but I suspect she'd move mountains for you. In fact, after meeting her brother, I believe the entire family would. You should have seen Zane bulldoze his way through the reporters. It was a sight to behold.'

It didn't take much imagination for Simon to see the picture Patsy had described. In fact, he remembered how the Mallorys had closed ranks around Lisa when Bryan had appeared on the scene and how they'd done the same for Andy.

'Be honest. If Mick were still alive, you'd go after her with your usual single-minded determination.'

'I would.'

'Then I hereby release you from worrying about me, from trying to solve my problems for me, from putting my needs before your own.'

'You can't do that!'

Patsy smiled. 'I just did. My therapist said this would be a liberating moment, and you know what? It is.' She leaned forward. 'Now, I want you to repeat after me. ''I will hereby pursue my own dreams and will not let Lisa slip through my fingers because I love her''.'

He rubbed the back of his neck. 'This is ridiculous.'

'What's ridiculous? That you love her?'

Hearing Patsy describe the feeling in his heart suddenly made it all too real. 'No. I love her more than anything, but I've screwed things up.'

'Christmas is a great time to correct past mistakes,' Patsy said softly. 'And, just so you'll know, you have my blessing. I couldn't have asked for a better woman for you to add to the family. If you need a Christmas hint—'

An idea suddenly took hold. 'I already have the perfect gift in mind. And the perfect way to give it.'

'Why is everyone so worried if I've packed enough bikinis?' Lisa complained to Savanna a week later at the clinic's annual lavish Christmas party. 'No one's asking you that question.'

Savanna added another elegant hors d'oeuvre to her plate. 'You're just being sensitive. Out of curiosity, how many skimpy numbers *did* you pack?'

'None. We aren't leaving until Monday. I have lots of time to throw a few things in a suitcase.'

'My, my, we're testy these days. Where's your Christmas cheer?'

'It got up and left,' Lisa grumbled, glaring at Zane who

was seated at Simon's front-and-center table, next to Patsy and the Beningtons. Her own brother was fraternizing with the enemy. She had half a notion to return his Christmas gifts and substitute a lump of coal in his stocking.

'Too bad you and Simon broke up. You made a nice couple.'

'We did *not* break up. You can't break something that was never together.' She rubbed her temples, feeling the start of another tension headache. She'd had a lot of them in recent days.

'Yeah, right.'

'It's true. I was just a babysitter for a while. Now that Patsy's here, I'm not needed.' In more ways than one, she thought glumly.

'I know it's been a let-down for you,' Savanna said kindly, 'but you'll regain your perspective after this cruise. Trust me. Speaking of our little vacation, you look stunning in that dress you bought for the Captain's Ball. If the married men can't take their eyes off you tonight—I've seen them ogling you—think of the handsome dudes you'll attract on board ship.'

Lisa smoothed her hands along the ivory satin formal she'd chosen. The low-cut bodice was daring in her opinion, especially since the garment only had spaghetti straps to hold it in place, but she had to admit that she filled it out nicely in the right places.

'Yeah, well, this dress should be in my suitcase right now, instead of risking a spill,' Lisa muttered. She glanced around the room, wishing the live band would stop playing so Alice could present the gifts and she could go home.

'Why didn't you ever tell me who Simon's sister is?'

'It wasn't important.'

'Not important? My goodness, we know an honest-to-goodness celebrity. How long is she staying in town?'

'Through New Year.' She'd made a point not to ask any personal questions, but Simon had dropped that tidbit when she'd asked about Kyle and Courtney. Patsy's psychologist had apparently agreed that she'd made enough progress to warrant outpatient visits rather than inpatient care.

Alice sauntered to the center of the postage-stamp-sized dance floor and waited for the noise to die down, while Roger wheeled a cart containing brightly wrapped packages to the front.

'Finally,' Lisa grumbled, as she and Savanna returned to their seats at a table near the exit.

'While the band takes a short break,' Alice began, 'we'd like to take this opportunity to give the physicians tokens of our appreciation for a great year.'

Lisa blocked out the rest of Alice's speech as she focused on Simon. It should be illegal for a man to be so handsome in a tux, she thought. Watching him glide across the dance floor with SueEllen had brought a lump to her throat. If she hadn't hitched a ride with Savanna, she would have left right then and there.

One by one, Alice called the doctors forward and Roger handed them their packages. Each one opened his or her box in full view of everyone, before saying a few words.

Alice called Simon's name last. Lisa couldn't take her eyes off him as he strode forward to receive the gift she had agonized over for weeks.

A collective gasp resounded through the hotel's dining room as he held the ship aloft. The glass sparkled like diamonds as he twisted and turned the work of art for all to see.

'I'll treasure this always,' he told the crowd, clearly touched, 'because I know how much thought went into the purchase of this gift. You see, it has a special meaning to me, a special meaning of dreams and the storms one must pass through to attain them.'

Tears threatened, but Lisa didn't have any trouble noticing how Simon's gaze fell directly on her, as if he'd kept tabs on her whereabouts all evening.

He moved toward his chair and handed the ship to Patsy. Without waiting to see what would happen next, Lisa sprang to her feet.

'Let's go,' she told Savanna with false brightness. 'Party's over.'

'Not yet,' Savanna whispered. 'Sit down while I find my shoes.'

Simon returned to front and center. 'If you'll bear with me, I'd like to make a special presentation, too.'

Lisa slowly sank into her chair, bemoaning her delayed escape.

'During my short time in Farmington, I've come to depend on a lot of different people. They include my colleagues, who are not only good friends but also professionals I can rely upon. The clerical staff who keep the red tape in our lives relatively tangle-free.' The crowd twittered.

'I should also mention the support staff in our lab and X-ray departments who go the extra mile when I want something done yesterday.' He grinned as the audience chuckled again.

As before, his gaze fixed directly on Lisa and she shivered under its intensity. Her nerves seemed on edge as she waited for his next remarks.

'I have a special gift for the person I've come to know so well these past few weeks. Maybe you can guess who I'm talking about.'

Lisa's heart seemed to skip a beat and she alternated between feeling cold dread and warm anticipation.

'She's trustworthy, spirited and never lets me intimidate her.'

'Sounds like my dog,' someone shouted. The crowd burst into laughter.

Simon managed a grin, but didn't break eye contact. 'She's kind, and generous, and is like a breath of fresh air wherever she goes.'

A few people at nearby tables turned to smile at her. Someone whispered her name, but she was too mesmerized to notice who had spoken.

'She means a lot to me and I can't imagine the future without her. I love her and want to marry her.'

Lisa could have heard a pin drop in the momentary silence. The whisper turned to a low murmur. The guests all turned to stare at her, their faces wreathed in smiles as they nodded their approval.

'I'm asking her to share this gift with me, in sickness and in health, for richer for poorer. My special gift is for—'

'Lisa,' the crowd chanted.

With a plea in his eyes but his face otherwise unreadable, Simon slowly extended his right hand, palm up. In spite of his confidence, she sensed his apprehension as he waited for her acceptance or rejection.

Lisa was stunned. She'd never believed that he would change his mind and ask her into his tight family circle, much less do so in such a flamboyant manner. Knowing how much he valued his privacy, he had risked her refusal in the presence of the entire clinic staff.

Savanna nudged her. 'Go on. He admitted he loves you in front of everybody. What more do you want?'

Somehow her wobbly knees managed to hold her as she rose. With each step forward, the wariness in Simon's eyes turned to joy and his smile inched across his face until his whole countenance shone.

She slipped her hand into his and the crowd instantly quieted.

The warmth of his touch gave her confidence and emphasized the rightness of her decision.

Someone hollered out, 'What's the gift?'

Simon reached into his right breast pocket and pulled out an envelope containing two tickets. 'A honeymoon.'

He lowered his voice for Lisa's ears only. 'If it's OK with you, I'm taking Savanna's place on your cruise.'

She gasped, then turned to stare at her friend who was beaming like a lighthouse beacon.

Lisa faced him, hoping the tears of joy in her eyes wouldn't spill down her cheeks. 'Oh, Simon. I don't know what to say.'

'Say yes,' Roger shouted.

'The question is, do you want a honeymoon for Christmas?' he asked.

Lisa flung her arms around his neck and breathed in his familiar scent. 'More than anything.'

Suddenly Simon's lips met hers and she was so happy she could have sworn her feet left the ground.

Cheers and stomping feet echoed through the room as even those at the back of the room understood her answer. Before she could gather her wits, Simon broke off the kiss and ushered her through the throng of well-wishers to the door and the small, unoccupied coat room.

For lack of a place to sit, he lifted her onto the counter and enfolded her in a loose embrace.

'We can't organize everything before Monday,' she said, thinking of the huge task ahead of them. 'I don't have a dress, a cake or a minister.'

'I have a confession,' he said, his eyes reflecting insecurity. 'I pulled some strings and traded your tickets in for

December 26th instead of the 22nd. We can have a Christmas ceremony.'

'I'd like that,' she said softly.

'Savanna's taking you shopping first thing in the morning, although the dress you're wearing looks great to me.' He grinned as his gaze traveled over her gown. 'I've already ordered flowers and arranged for a minister. If we get our marriage license on Monday, we'll be set.'

'You really have been busy,' she said in wonderment.

'The women of our family—your mom, Jill, Mary and Patsy—have decided to host a reception for us when we return, complete with cake and mints and whatever other goodies you want.'

She was amazed at what he'd done. 'How long have you been planning this?'

He wore a boyish grin and shrugged. 'A few days.'

'And tonight? How did you manage it?'

'Savanna was the only one who knew. Everyone else was as surprised as you were.'

Lisa stared into his face. 'What made you change your mind? I thought you didn't—'

'You made me start thinking about where I'd been and where I was going. My future looked terribly lonely without you.'

'What about Patsy and—?'

'It took a while, but I realized you were right. Patsy shouldn't depend solely on me. I have to let go so she can stand on her own feet. If she needs us, we'll be there—and your family. I'm sorry it took me such a long time to learn the lesson.'

'Oh, Simon.' She rubbed at her nose and wished for a handkerchief.

'Your sense of duty is as strong as mine,' he continued. 'If and when Patsy wants our help, we'll *all* be there for her. Together. A cord of two strands is stronger than a cord of one.'

He gave her a lazy grin. 'So, the-future-Mrs-Travers, how do you feel about Christmas now?'

She leaned forward to accept his kiss. 'It's become my favorite holiday.'

MILLS & BOON®

Makes any time special™

Mills & Boon publish 29 new titles every month. Select from...

Modern Romance™   **Tender Romance**™

Sensual Romance™

Medical Romance™ **Historical Romance**™

MAT2

The perfect gift this Christmas from

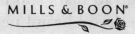

FREE

4 BOOKS
AND A SURPRISE GIFT!

We would like to take this opportunity to thank you for reading this Mills & Boon® book by offering you the chance to take FOUR more specially selected titles from the Medical Romance™ series absolutely FREE! We're also making this offer to introduce you to the benefits of the Reader Service™—

    ★ FREE home delivery   ★ FREE gifts and competitions
    ★ FREE monthly Newsletter   ★ Exclusive Reader Service discounts
        ★ Books available before they're in the shops

Accepting these FREE books and gift places you under no obligation to buy; you may cancel at any time, even after receiving your free shipment. Simply complete your details below and return the entire page to the address below. *You don't even need a stamp!*

YES! Please send me 4 free Medical Romance books and a surprise gift. I understand that unless you hear from me, I will receive 6 superb new titles every month for just £2.40 each, postage and packing free. I am under no obligation to purchase any books and may cancel my subscription at any time. The free books and gift will be mine to keep in any case.

M0ZEC

Ms/Mrs/Miss/Mr ....Initials ....
BLOCK CAPITALS PLEASE
Surname ....
Address ....

....
....Postcode ....

Send this whole page to:
UK: FREEPOST CN81, Croydon, CR9 3WZ
EIRE: PO Box 4546, Kilcock, County Kildare (stamp required)